FOLLOW THE CODES . . .

Join Art and Camille in viewing famous paintings with the interactive QR codes feature you'll discover in these pages.

To access the paintings you will need a smartphone or tablet and a connection to the Internet. If you don't have a QR reader app on your device, ask a parent or guardian to download a free QR reader from the app store. Once you have downloaded the app, simply open it and hover the device over the QR code, which looks like this:

The art will appear in your browser.

The QR codes simply provide a link to a museum's website. If you don't have access to a QR reader or if a link expires, be sure to visit the website directly. The websites include the National Gallery of Art (www.nga.gov), the Art Institute of Chicago (www.artic.edu), the Metropolitan Museum of Art (www.metmusem.org), and—of course—the Isabella Stewart Gardner Museum (www.gardnermuseum.org). Happy sleuthing!

The Rembrandt Conspiracy

DERON HICKS

A LOST ART MYSTERY

HOUGHTON MIFFLIN HARCOURT

BOSTON NEW YORK

hmhbooks.com

The text was set in Weiss.
Design by Natalie Fondriest and Whitney Leader-Picone

The Library of Congress has cataloged the hardcover edition as follows:
Names: Hicks, Deron R., author.
Title: The Rembrandt conspiracy / by Deron R. Hicks.
Description: Boston ; New York : Houghton Mifflin Harcourt, [2020] |
Series: The lost art mysteries | Companion to: The Van Gogh deception. |
Audience: Ages 10 to 12. | Audience: Grades 4–6. |
Summary: "Art and Camille team up once again to solve a large museum theft, using one of the biggest heists in history to help them solve the case." — Provided by publisher.
Identifiers: LCCN 2019050628 (print) | LCCN 2019050629 (ebook) |
Subjects: CYAC: Mystery and detective stories. | National Portrait Gallery (Smithsonian Institution) — Fiction. | Art thefts — Fiction. |
Washington (D.C.) — Fiction.
Classification: LCC PZ7.H531615 Rem 2020 (print) |
LCC PZ7.H531615 (ebook) | DDC [Fic] — dc23
LC record available at https://lccn.loc.gov/2019050628
LC ebook record available at https://lccn.loc.gov/2019050629

ISBN: 978-0-358-25621-2 hardcover
ISBN: 978-0-358-56976-3 paperback

Manufactured in the United States of America
1 2021
4500831942

Dedicated to my grandfather J. C. Parker (1897–1990),
for whom life was an adventure and tall tales were
simply part of the journey

NATIONAL PORTRAIT GALLERY

WASHINGTON DC

1st Floor

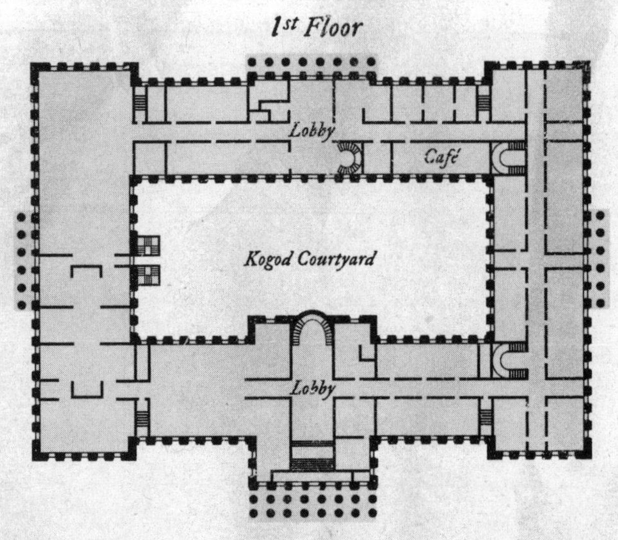

2nd Floor

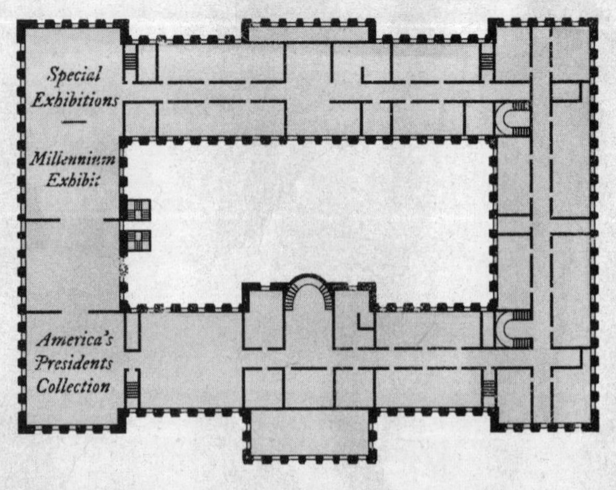

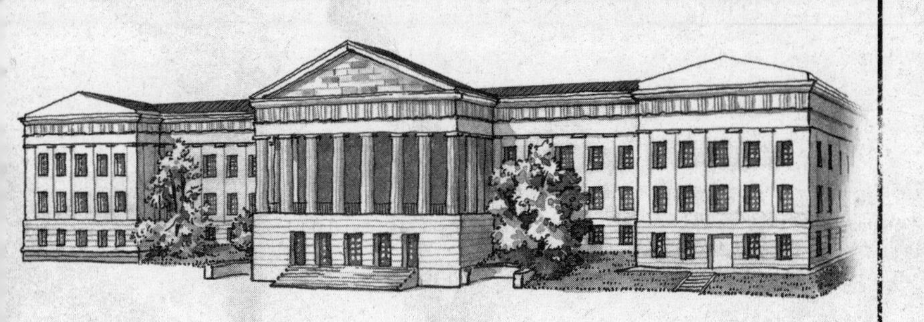

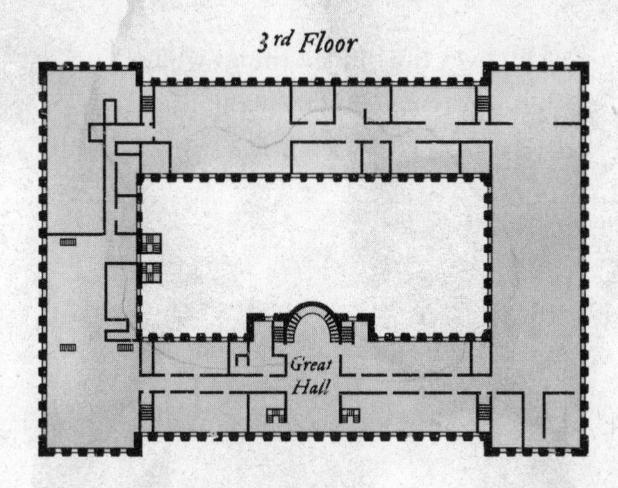
3rd Floor
Great Hall

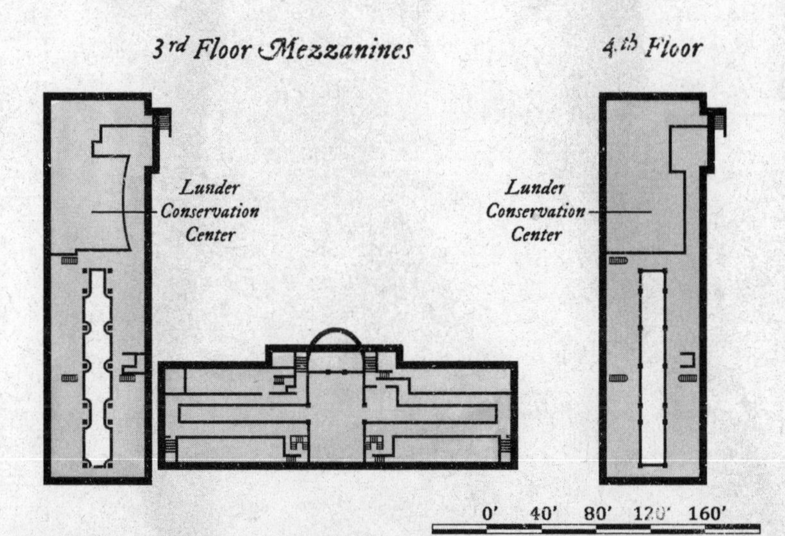
3rd Floor Mezzanines
4th Floor
Lunder Conservation Center
Lunder Conservation Center
0' 40' 80' 120' 160'

Discover the hidden things which
you now inquire about.

—Rembrandt van Rijn

PROLOGUE

EIGHTY-ONE MINUTES

2:00 a.m.

Thirty years ago

Boston, Massachusetts

Sam checked his watch—a classic chronograph with a tan leather band. It had been owned by his father and may have been scuffed up a bit over the years, but it was always reliable.

The watch confirmed what Sam already knew—it was time.

He winced as he forced himself to gulp down the last bit of coffee. It was ice cold and bitter. Sam hated cold coffee, but he needed all the caffeine he could get. It had been a long night—and it was far from over.

The sounds of St. Patrick's Day revelers in the distance drifted through the open window of the nondescript red car in which Sam sat. And despite the late hour, he knew that the holiday festivities would carry on well into the early morning. Fortunately, the quiet tree-lined street on which he was parked would be free of celebrations.

Sam rolled up the window of the car. He turned the

rearview mirror toward himself and adjusted his cap. A slight smile creased his face. The irony of wearing the cap was not lost on him.

"Ready?" Sam asked the large man in a police uniform sitting next to him.

"Ready," Bob replied.

Sam—who also wore a police officer's uniform—knew, of course, that the man sitting next to him was not actually named Bob. Nor, for that matter, was Sam's name actually Sam. That was the nature of their business—no real names. It was better that way. It was easier that way.

The men stepped out of the car and paused. The cool night air felt refreshing. A light fog was just beginning to settle in around them, and the mist formed halos of light around the street lamps lining the narrow lane. Sam glanced around. There was no one in sight. He had spent several weeks driving in and around the area at night, so the lack of people was not a surprise—it was an expectation. He knew the area and its patterns well. It was surrounded by two parks and several colleges and universities. At this time of night, it was about as quiet a place as anyone could find in the city—even with the festivities that were currently under way.

Sam recognized every vehicle on the street. The blue van that was always parked across the street at night. The small black car a little farther back down the lane—always parked too far away from the curb—and the white midsize car backed into a short driveway near the intersection.

There was a gray cat that patrolled the area—he usually slept beneath a mailbox on the corner. The only person who ever appeared this late was an older man who liked to walk his small brown dog just after midnight. The dog's name was Millie. Millie had already made her appearance and returned home for the night. The area—including the cat and Millie—was predictable, and nothing appeared out of place this evening.

"Nice night," Bob said.

"Perfect night," Sam replied.

Sam grabbed his satchel from the back seat, locked the car, and followed Bob up the sidewalk. As they walked, Sam continued to scan the street for anything that appeared out of place. It was the details that mattered—the little things that most people take for granted. In his job, those details mattered. Details were the difference between success and failure.

Moments later Sam and Bob found themselves standing in front of a green door on the side of a massive brick building. The building itself, at least from the exterior, was fairly nondescript—four stories of tan brick walls and dark paned windows. It could have easily been mistaken for a simple apartment building or an office complex. However, it was—in fact—an Italian villa located in the heart of the city. Sam paused for a moment to admire the grand palace. It would be the last time he would ever see it.

Too bad, he thought—he really liked the building. It was unique, and he liked unique. He had spent a lot of time over the past few weeks walking the corridors and climbing the stairways of the grand palace. He knew every corner of the building—the large halls, the small side rooms, the narrow passages, and the alcoves. He knew how the light filtered through its windows in the morning, and he had seen the building's magnificent courtyard in the deep shadows of the late afternoon. The building seemed to exist outside the confines of the modern world. It was a wonderful, kaleidoscope-like view of the past—a jumble of centuries piled into one building. It was all very beautiful.

Sam sighed.

He was getting old. He didn't used to be so sentimental.

Bob pushed the button on the intercom next to the door.

Moments later a tall young man with long hair appeared in the glass window at the doorway. He wore a security guard's uniform, his shirt untucked and unbuttoned.

The young man's voice crackled through the intercom.

"Can I help you, officers?"

"We've had a report of a disturbance in the building's courtyard," Bob explained.

"Probably just some kids celebrating St. Patty's Day," Sam added. "But we need to check it out."

The young man seemed confused. "I didn't hear anything," he said. "Are you sure?"

"Listen, kid," Sam replied. "I didn't hear anything either, okay? And I'm not sure how anyone could have gotten into the courtyard. But someone reported that they heard something, and our job is to check it out. How about not giving us a hard time tonight? Just let us in, we take a quick look, and then we're gone—okay?"

The young man hesitated for a moment, the uncertainty clear in his face. Finally, he shrugged. "Sure. I guess better safe than sorry."

He retreated to a security desk within an office across the room. Seconds later there was a slight buzz followed by a clicking sound as the door unlocked. Bob opened the door and stepped inside. Sam took one last look around and then followed Bob into the small security office. He pulled the door shut behind him.

"The courtyard's that way," the young man said from behind the security desk. "Just down the hallway. You can't miss it." He pointed toward a door to his right.

"Thanks," Sam replied. "We'll just check it . . ."

Sam paused. He stared intently at the young man.

"Don't I know you?" he asked.

The young man shook his head. "I don't think so," he replied nervously.

"I'm almost positive I know you," Sam said. "Could you step out from behind the desk, please?"

The young man did as he was asked—as Sam expected he would.

Sam turned to Bob. "Does he look familiar to you?"

Bob rubbed his chin thoughtfully. "He looks very familiar," he replied.

Sam snapped his fingers. "I've got it," he said. "There's a warrant out for your arrest."

The young man's eyes went wide and his jaw dropped open. "M-my arrest?" he stammered. "No, sir—there has to be some sort of a mistake. I swear I haven't done anything."

"It's not a mistake," Sam said as he pulled a set of handcuffs from his belt. "Now turn around and place your hands on the wall."

Once more, the young man did as he was instructed. Sam could feel the young man's hands shaking as Sam pulled his arms behind his back and handcuffed him. The young man appeared to be on the verge of hyperventilating.

"What's going on here?" a voice called from the doorway on the other side of the room. It was another man dressed in a security guard uniform—a bit older with far less hair.

"Your coworker has an outstanding warrant for his arrest," Sam explained.

"A warrant?" the security guard said. "Well, that's just great. Seriously, do you have to arrest him now? He's only got a few more hours on his shift—can't he turn himself in or something?"

"It's about to get even better," Bob said. He pulled out another set of handcuffs. Moments later the second security guard was also handcuffed and facing the wall next to his long-haired coworker. Bob nodded to Sam and left the office.

"You're not really police officers, are you?" the young man asked.

Sam couldn't help but smile. "That would be correct."

The young man's breathing was becoming labored. Sam didn't need a medical emergency. That wasn't part of the plan. He needed to calm the kid down.

Sam patted the young man on the back. "Don't worry, kid," he said. "Just cooperate and you'll be fine."

"There are more guards in the building," the other security guard blurted out. "If you leave now, you can probably still get away. They'll be here any minute."

"There are no more security guards," Sam replied calmly. "Just the two of you."

"And there's a silent alarm," the older guard said, the desperation now evident in his voice. "I activated it, and the police will be here any minute."

Sam had to give it to the guy—he was certainly trying.

"There is a silent alarm," Sam responded. "The alarm button sits beneath the left corner of the security desk. I can assure you that it has not been activated. And before you ask, I am also fully aware of the building's security cameras and motion detectors. My partner is—at this very moment

—disabling the entire system and removing the videotapes."

Sam paused for a moment.

"Anything else you would care to add?" he finally asked.

Neither security guard spoke—it was clear that both of them now understood exactly what was happening.

"Excellent," Sam said. "And while I have enjoyed the pleasantries we have exchanged, my colleague and I have business to attend to this evening."

Sam made his way out of the security office, down a short corridor, and up a set of stone stairs to the second floor. He then headed directly to a large room in the southwest corner of the building. The light in the room was dim, but it made little difference—a glow practically radiated from the object on the wall. Sam could smell the sea air and feel the cool mist against his face. He could sense the men's struggle and fear as the waves crashed around them. He could hear the crack of the wooden beams, the ropes snapping, and the sails flapping in the wind.

It was breathtaking.

"Hello, my friend," Sam said. "I've come for you."

CHAPTER 1

4:23 p.m.

Friday, March 25

National Portrait Gallery, Washington, DC

Camille Sullivan brushed a long strand of curly red hair from her face and squinted at the elderly gentleman on the far side of the room. Arthur Hamilton Jr.—known to his friends and family simply as Art—stood next to Camille. And though barely a year older at twelve years of age, he towered almost a foot over her—not including the mound of bright red hair that flew off in all directions from the top of her head. However, neither the difference in age nor in height was of any concern to Camille.

"That old guy is staring at us," Camille insisted. "It's weird."

"He's not staring at us," Art replied.

"Is he wearing a beret?" Camille asked. "He's way too old to wear a beret. I'm just saying it's not a good look for him. It's like he's trying to be French or something. Is he French? I guess he could be French, but it's still not a good look."

"He's not French," Art replied. "He's actually from the

Netherlands—and he's not too old for a beret. I actually think he looks good in it."

"And check out that mustache or goatee or whatever is on his face," Camille continued. "He thinks he is so cool. I'm telling you, it's just plain weird."

Art was in no mood to argue with Camille. "Fine," he said. "He's staring at us, and the mustache is weird."

"And what's he wearing?" Camille whispered. "Look at him—he's got his collar all flipped up."

"I don't know what he's wearing. Why does it matter?"

"It doesn't," Camille said. "I'm just saying he's way too old to be doing that."

Art rolled his eyes. "He's not trying to be cool," he said. "He's just sitting there."

"I like his hair, though," Camille said.

Art smiled. "I thought you might."

The dark beret sitting on top of the older man's head could not contain the curly gray hair that billowed out like clouds from the sides of the man's head. The man's hair seemed to have a life of its own—just like Camille's.

"But I still think he's staring at us," Camille insisted once more.

Art waved at his father, who stood on the far side of the room next to the elderly man in the beret. Art was the spitting image of his father—tall, blond, and slender. Arthur Hamilton Sr. motioned them over—an introduction to the older gentleman was apparently in order. And a brief respite from Camille's commentary was more than welcome.

"I'm nervous," Camille said as they made their way across the room.

"Why?" Art asked.

"You said he's worth more than a hundred million dollars," Camille replied. "That's a bunch of money."

Art shrugged. He had been around people like the man in the beret his entire life. He had met some that were worth even more. He was used to it.

"Camille! Art!" Arthur Hamilton Sr. exclaimed as they arrived by his side, a broad smile across his face.

"Hello, Dr. Hamilton," Camille replied.

"Hey, Dad," Art said.

"How was school today?" Arthur Hamilton Sr. asked. It was always the first question he asked after school. It was sort of annoying.

"All good," Art replied. He had learned from experience that the shorter the answer, the better.

"It was okay," Camille added. "You know—it was school."

She peeked around Dr. Hamilton at the man in the beret.

"We just wanted to stop by and see how things were going," Art said. "How's the patient?"

"Well," Art's dad replied as he turned toward the older

gentleman, "I'd say he's doing pretty well for someone who is more than three hundred and fifty years old."

Arthur Hamilton Sr. stood beside his son and Camille in a large room on the second floor of a massive stone building located between F Street and G Street in downtown Washington, DC. The building, which traced back to 1836, occupied two full city blocks—the massive stone columns of its southern façade faced directly down Eighth Street toward the National Archives. Its thick granite walls had hosted President Abraham Lincoln's second inaugural ball, had provided housing for troops during the Civil War, and had been the home of the United States Patent Office for decades. A large gallery within the building had been—for a brief period of time—the largest enclosed space in the entire United States. But the building eventually fell into disrepair and disuse, its history and contributions to the country seemingly forgotten by the very city it had served for so long. Demolition seemed inevitable—a parking deck had been slated to take its place. Fortunately, the Smithsonian Institution stepped in to save the historic landmark, and on October 7, 1968, the doors of the grand building reopened to a new purpose—the National Portrait Gallery.

The National Portrait Gallery was founded by the United States Congress for the purpose of displaying paintings of Americans who have made significant contributions to the history and culture of the United States. Its galleries were filled with portraits of Americans who defined the country—great artists, musicians, film stars, athletes, politicians, civil rights leaders, socialites, activists, and many others. However, within the west wing of the building was a related and yet very distinct set of operations: the Lunder Conservation Center. The scientists, conservationists, and technicians of the Lunder Center were responsible for caring for the artwork owned by the entire Smithsonian Institution—a collection of virtually unlimited historic, artistic, and economic value. Experts within the center repaired and restored paintings, statues, photographs, drawings, and prints. There was even a frame conservation studio in which historic picture frames were carefully cared for and preserved. It was a weighty responsibility to lead the Lunder Center but a task that well suited Arthur Hamilton Sr. as the recently appointed director of the facility.

Dr. Hamilton's path to the Lunder Center had taken him across the globe. He had long been considered one of the premier art conservation scientists in the world, but he had spent most of his professional life—and all of his son's life—constantly moving from one job to the next. His unique skills were in high demand, and Dr. Hamilton had seen little need to settle down in one location. Even following his wife's untimely death when Art was only four years of age, Dr. Hamilton had carried on as always—albeit with his young son as his constant travel companion. They had lived for months at a time in Paris, London, Shanghai, Los Angeles, Rome, and Cape Town. Dr. Hamilton had educated his son the best that he could—his classroom was whatever apartment, park, museum, or coffee shop happened to be convenient.

And what an education it had been. Art had spent most of his life hanging around with artists, authors, academics, presidents, poets, and monarchs. He and his father had spent nights in castles and once had a picnic on the top of Westminster Cathedral in London. Art spoke fluent French, read voraciously, and knew more about art than the directors at most museums. Dr. Hamilton had walked with his son among the ruins of the Roman Forum. They had visited Shakespeare's grave. They had stood on the Great Wall of China. Art had seen the world, and Dr. Hamilton was proud of the education he had managed to provide him. And he was proud of his son—the boy was smart, caring, and resourceful. Everything had seemed to be going well—until suddenly it wasn't.

Just three months earlier, Art had found himself alone in Washington, DC, with amnesia—no knowledge of who he was or how he had come to be there. Dr. Hamilton, unbeknownst to his son, had been kidnapped—he had feared he would never see Art again. But the boy had overcome the failings of his own memory to save Dr. Hamilton and prevent one of the greatest art frauds of all time—with the help of his remarkable red-haired friend Camille. It had been an incredible feat for a person of any age, let alone a twelve-year-old boy and his eleven-year-old friend. Following those events, it would have been easy to simply fall back into their same routine—back on the road to yet another country, another museum, another job. However, those same fateful events had convinced Dr. Hamilton that there was one thing he had never truly provided for his son—a home. Dr. Hamilton had come to realize that a home was so much more than simply a house—it was a connection to a place, a community, and a people. A home is part of a person's very identity—and it was identity that his son had struggled so hard to find after losing his memory. Perhaps, Dr. Hamilton thought, the lack of a home had hampered his son's efforts to overcome amnesia and find himself. He ultimately decided it was time to settle down. It was time to find their home.

The Smithsonian Institution had jumped at the chance to hire someone of Dr. Hamilton's credentials and experience to lead the Lunder Center—and his son had, in turn, jumped at the chance to attend a real school (and have real friends) for once in his life. They had purchased a small house near Camille and her mother, Mary, and quickly settled into life in Washington, DC.

CHAPTER 2

4:28 p.m.

Friday, March 25

National Portrait Gallery, Washington, DC

Dr. Hamilton gestured to the painting mounted on the wall of the National Portrait Gallery. In the painting an older man glanced past his left shoulder, his gaze directly engaging the viewer. There were bags under his eyes. His brow was furrowed, and his face was lined with wrinkles. He wore a dark beret, his gray hair sweeping out from beneath.

"Camille," he said, "I would like to introduce you to Rembrandt van Rijn—the most famous Dutch artist in history, and one of the most famous in the entire history of the world. He painted this self-portrait in 1659 when he was around fifty-three years old."

Camille dropped her school bag on the floor and leaned in to get a closer look at the painting. She remembered seeing Rembrandt's self-portrait at the National Gallery of Art in DC, but this was the closest she had ever been to a painting this old or this famous. The painting was exceptionally dark—burnt umber and

deep shadows dominated the canvas. The sole exception was Rembrandt's face, which seemed to glow with some sort of strange internal light.

Camille remembered what Art had told her on the walk over from school. Rembrandt had painted a ton of portraits of other people, but he was particularly well known for his self-portraits. He had created more than forty of them during the course of his life, completing his first self-portrait when he was only twenty-two years old, the last when he was sixty-three years old, the same year he died. Art had also mentioned that a self-portrait by Rembrandt could be worth more than a hundred million dollars, perhaps more. It made Camille nervous to be so close to something so expensive. What if she accidentally sneezed on it? She had no idea what snot could do to a painting that old, but it couldn't be good. And just thinking about it made her nose start to twitch. Camille slowly backed away from the painting.

"So what do you think?" Art's father asked.

"He seems sad," Camille said.

"And for good reason," Dr. Hamilton replied. "Although Rembrandt was a famous painter in the Netherlands, the last few years of his life were tough—he was forced to sell all of his possessions and had a hard time paying his bills. He actually ended up being buried in an unmarked grave because no one could afford to pay for a proper burial for him."

Camille nodded. The face that looked back at her from

the self-portrait seemed to capture all of that. She could see the frustration and the pain etched in his expression. She wondered what Rembrandt had been thinking about as he painted the self-portrait.

"Anything else catch your attention?" Dr. Hamilton asked.

"The paint," Camille replied. "It's so thick." It was almost as if tubes of paint had been squeezed straight onto the canvas and then pushed around with a brush. She had seen other paintings that seemed as smooth as glass—she could hardly tell that a paintbrush had been used. But the Rembrandt self-portrait had peaks and valleys and swirls and twists of thick paint. He had used the paint to create the wrinkles on his face and the beads that lined his beret. She could see every brush stroke. It was all pretty incredible.

"The thick paint is a style called impasto," Art said. "It means 'dough' in Italian. Rembrandt was the master of the technique."

"I'm glad we managed to get this painting for the exhibit," Dr. Hamilton said." You can't have a portrait exhibit this big without a Rembrandt."

"What exhibit?" Camille asked.

Arthur Hamilton Sr. looked at his son. "You didn't tell her about the Millennium Exhibit?"

"I didn't want to ruin the surprise," Art replied.

Dr. Hamilton turned to Camille. "It's the most important exhibit the National Portrait Gallery has ever hosted," he explained. "A collection of the most important portraits ever painted—works by Rembrandt, Vermeer, Degas, Manet, Whistler, Diego Rivera, and Mary Cassatt. There's even a portrait of Shakespeare that will be arriving soon from England, and an Egyptian mummy portrait."

A mummy portrait? Camille had never heard of such a thing.

"Dad's job is to protect the paintings while they are here," Art said.

"He's guarding the paintings?" Camille asked. She thought Art's dad was some sort of scientist, not a security guard.

"Not exactly," Dr. Hamilton replied. "We have a security team that takes care of that—and trust me, this exhibit hall will have the best security known to mankind. Lasers, motion detectors, facial recognition software, regular cameras, infrared cameras—all the works. And every square inch of the room will be monitored twenty-four hours a day from a security room in the basement. No one will be able to get past the security in this room."

It all sounded very impressive.

"So then," Camille asked, "exactly what are you protecting the paintings from?"

"You," Dr. Hamilton said.

"Me?" Camille replied. She edged even farther back from the self-portrait of Rembrandt.

"Actually, I'm protecting the paintings from all of us —me, you, Art . . . Everybody."

Things were not getting any clearer.

Arthur Hamilton Sr. continued. "There will be almost a billion dollars' worth of paintings in this exhibit, most of them loaned to the National Portrait Gallery by other museums. Every one of the paintings is irreplaceable, and most of them are very old and fragile. My job is to make sure that they aren't damaged while they are under our care. I have to make sure that they don't get too hot or too cold. I have to make sure that the air is just right. I have to make sure the lights don't cause any damage. I have to make sure that the humidity in the exhibition hall is absolutely perfect—not too dry and not too moist. And I have to make sure that all of that happens while thousands of people just like you are walking through the room every day."

"Why do the people make a difference?" Camille asked.

"Excellent question," Dr. Hamilton replied. He turned to his son. "Art, why do people make a difference?"

"What's the normal temperature for a human?" Art asked Camille.

Her mother had a thermometer that she touched to her forehead every time she thought Camille was getting sick.

"And if it was ninety-eight point six degrees outside right now," Art asked, "would it be hot or cold?"

That was a stupid question.

"Hot," Camille replied. "It would be really hot."

"So what do you think happens when a thousand people who are that temperature get together in a room?" Art asked.

Oh, Camille thought.

"The room gets hotter," she replied.

"Exactly," said Dr. Hamilton. "And that's not all. The air we breathe out is carbon dioxide—and it's warm and full of moisture. Microbes love that, and the wrong microbes can slowly destroy a painting."

"So people are bad for paintings," Camille said. It almost seemed foolish to put paintings worth a billion dollars into a room with those types of risks.

"Sort of," replied Dr. Hamilton. "But these paintings were not intended to rest in some closet. They were intended to be seen—to be appreciated."

"So how do you protect them?" asked Camille. She imagined large glass boxes covering each painting.

Dr. Hamilton pulled a small white object from his pocket and handed it to Camille. "With this," he said.

Camille examined the device—it was about the size of a credit card and perhaps a quarter of an inch thick. The only distinguishing features were two small holes on the edge of the device. It didn't seem very impressive at all—not nearly as impressive as the security cameras, lasers, and facial recognition software.

"So what is it?" she asked.

"Technically, it's a HTAQ-23Z module," Art's father replied, "but I call it Soteria after the Greek goddess of protection. It measures the temperature of the room, the humidity in the air, the intensity of the light, and the air quality. There are hundreds of Soteria positioned around the room—along the ceiling, on the baseboards, around the windows. They are everywhere."

"So what happens if something goes wrong?" Camille asked.

Dr. Hamilton pulled out his phone and held it up. "All of that information is constantly being sent to my phone. If anything goes wrong, Soteria will notify me immediately, and the system will automatically start making adjustments. The system can filter the air, change the temperature in the room, adjust the lights, and make any other changes necessary to keep the room just perfect for the paintings."

Camille was impressed. It wasn't quite as cool as the lasers and facial recognition software, but it was still pretty impressive. And it was named after a Greek goddess—so it had that going for it as well.

Dr. Hamilton turned to Art. "I guess since you didn't tell Camille about the exhibit, you also didn't mention the other thing?"

Art shook his head. "Not yet."

"Perhaps you should tell her about the other thing."

Art shrugged his shoulders. "I guess," he said. "But what if she's not interested in the other thing?"

"What other thing?" Camille interrupted.

"It's really not a big deal," said Art.

"Then what is it?" Camille demanded. She was growing impatient.

"There's going to be a big gala here at the museum the night before the exhibit opens," Art said. "Dad thought you and your mom might want to come, but it's just going to be a lot of people in tuxedos and fancy dresses. Boring stuff. Not very exciting. I told him you probably wouldn't be interested."

"Ugh," Camille said. "No thank you." The thought of putting on a dress and hanging out with a bunch of adults did not sound the least bit exciting.

"That's what I thought," Art said. "I mean, so what if the Queen of England is going to be here, right?"

Wait—what?

"The Queen of England?" Camille exclaimed. "The actual Queen of England? Elizabeth II? The one that lives in England in Buckingham Palace? She's going to be here . . . in the museum?"

In the past couple of years the news had been filled with stories about royal weddings and royal births in England. And while she certainly knew all about William, Kate, Harry, and Meghan, it was the queen—Queen Elizabeth

—who really fascinated Camille. Camille had read that she had been Queen of England for more than sixty years—longer than any king or queen in the history of England.

A huge grin suddenly appeared on Art's face. "Yep," he said, "but if you don't want to come, I understand. You know, *ugh* and all that."

"I accept," she said. "Of course I want to come."

"Excellent," said Art's father. "It will be a night you'll never forget."

CHAPTER 3

3:53 p.m.
Tuesday, April 5
Sullivan residence, Washington, DC

Camille rushed inside and tossed her backpack to the floor in the foyer. She had a knot in her stomach that seemed to be growing bigger by the day.

"Mom!" she yelled. "Did it come?"

For the past week, Camille had anxiously waited for the invitation to the gala at the National Portrait Gallery to arrive in the mail. Art's father had told her that the invitations would be sent out "soon." Apparently Art's father had a very different definition of what "soon" meant than she did.

Ever since finding out that she was going to be invited, Camille had been obsessed. She had researched the correct way to greet the queen—just in case they were introduced. It had seemed fairly simple—she would be expected to curtsy and then address the queen as "Your Majesty." The curtsy seemed easy enough—bend your knees and bow your head at the same time. But despite watching several videos and practicing every night in front of a mirror, she always looked as if she were starting to faint or throw up. Graceful it was not.

But that was not the worst of her problems. Every day for the past week she had arrived home after school only to discover that the invitation had not yet been delivered. The doubts had immediately started to creep into her head.

Had Art's father changed his mind? After all, she was only eleven, and the gala would be filled with a lot of very important people. Did Art's father really want her hanging out with that crowd? Was he worried that she would embarrass him in front of the Queen of England? The more Camille thought about it, the more insecure she became.

Art, of course, had proved to be completely useless. They walked home together from school every day, and he always claimed that he had no clue as to when the invitations were going to be sent out.

Or does he? Maybe he was trying not to hurt her feelings. Maybe she really wasn't going to be invited, and Art already knew that.

The knot in her stomach grew tighter.

"Mom!" Camille yelled once more.

"I heard you the first time," Mary Sullivan said from upstairs. "I'm just finishing up a little work—be down in a minute."

In a minute? Camille's mother was a book editor—she spent her days reading manuscripts of new books, editing the manuscripts, and corresponding with authors across the globe. Camille understood that her mother worked from home, and Camille usually did her best to avoid disturbing her when she was busy. But this was different. Didn't her mom appreciate how anxious Camille was about the invitation? Didn't her mom understand the stress this was causing her daughter? Camille paced back and forth in the living room.

Finally, after what seemed like an eternity, Camille heard the sound of her mother's footsteps in the upstairs hallway. She rushed to the foyer to find her mother slowly descending the stairs carrying an armload of manuscripts. Her mother's dark brown hair had been pulled into a bun on the top of her head, and a red pen—the end of which had been chewed beyond recognition—was stuck over her right ear.

"How was school?" Mary Sullivan asked. "Do you have much homework?"

School?

Homework?

"Did it come?" Camille exclaimed.

Mary Sullivan smiled. "It came," she said as she dumped the stack of manuscripts onto a small table in the foyer. Camille immediately noticed the square white envelope resting on the top of the stack.

Camille grabbed the envelope and examined it closely. It had been addressed by hand to "Ms. Camille Sullivan and Guest" in a flowing, delicate script. On the back the words

National Portrait Gallery were embossed on the flap. The envelope felt thick and substantial, its importance seemingly built into the very fabric of the paper.

Camille carefully peeled back the flap and opened the envelope. Inside was a single square piece of paper—the invitation. She could feel her heart starting to race.

The Smithsonian Institution

would be honored by your presence

at a gala celebration of

THE MILLENNIUM EXHIBITION

April 23

From 6 p.m. to midnight

The National Portrait Gallery

Kogod Courtyard

Washington, DC

Formal attire

With grateful appreciation to our sponsor

The Hoggard Trust for the Arts

Camille ran her fingers across the words on the paper. She could feel the letters. Her mother had told her that really nice invitations were engraved—printed in a way that the letters were actually raised off the page. The invitation was simple but beautiful.

Camille looked at her mom. "This is going to be awesome."

Mary Sullivan nodded. "No doubt. And I assume I'm your guest—since I didn't get my own invitation?"

Camille paused as if in deep thought. "Perhaps," she finally said. "But what's in it for me?"

"Being allowed to go to the gala?" her mom replied. "How's that for a deal?"

All of the worry and anxiety over whether she would be invited had completely disappeared. She was going to attend one of the fanciest and most important events in all of Washington, DC. And possibly meet the Queen of England.

It couldn't get any better than that.

CHAPTER 4

4:37 p.m.

Thursday, April 14

National Portrait Gallery, Washington, DC

Day five, and Art—once more—lingered in the shadows. The people passing back and forth in front of him were little more than blurs—faceless and indistinguishable from one another. His hands twitched nervously at his sides.

Calm down, he told himself.

For four straight days he had simply watched.

He had thought of all sorts of possible explanations. He had run through a number of different scenarios. But the only answer that seemed to make any sense was the one that scared him the most.

He had told himself to give it another day. And then another.

Maybe—just maybe—he was wrong. That was possible. Maybe his imagination was simply running wild on him. And who could blame him? He had seen stuff—bad stuff. He knew that there were terrible people in the world. Maybe—just maybe—he was simply being paranoid. Maybe his mind was simply creating connections that weren't there.

But what if he wasn't wrong?

What if he wasn't being paranoid?

What if the pieces really did fit together?

He anticipated what he would say to his father—how he would explain what was going on. It wouldn't be easy, that was for sure.

Where would he even start in explaining what he had found?

The spilled mocha?

The forty-two steps?

Just the thought of trying to discuss this with his father gave him a headache. It wasn't as if his father didn't trust him. To the contrary, his father probably trusted him more than anyone else on the planet—and that was the problem. When someone placed that level of faith in you, it came with an obligation—an obligation to never abuse that trust. His father had just taken a new job—a job that might actually keep them in one place for more than a few months at a time. Art was attending a real school. He had real friends. He lived in a real house—not some cramped apartment or hotel. Art knew that he had to be careful. He couldn't just guess or speculate as to what was going to happen. He had to be one hundred percent positive, and then some. He couldn't afford to mess this opportunity up for his father. He couldn't afford to mess this up for himself.

And so, Art had decided on yet another day—day five.

In his heart Art knew what was going to take place.

His persistence was a matter of simply securing the evidence necessary to prove what he already knew to be true.

It had happened once before.

No one had expected it then—just like now.

No one had seen it coming.

But it had happened.

And if he was right, then this time it would be worse—far worse.

Art was determined that it would not happen again—at least while he could do something about it.

And so he lingered in the shadows for another day.

Day five.

CHAPTER 5

4:27 p.m.

Friday, April 15

National Portrait Gallery, Washington, DC

Camille stood in the lobby of the National Portrait Gallery and took a deep breath. She had not exactly lied to her mother about where she was going this afternoon—but she hadn't exactly told the truth, either. She had been to the Portrait Gallery several times with Art after school. And she had led her mom to believe that was what she was doing this afternoon. And she was—sort of.

For almost three straight months and with only limited exceptions, Art had walked home with Camille after school each day. It wasn't something they had ever planned to do—it had just happened. They would meet in the courtyard in front of school and make the five-block walk to the street on which they both lived. It was nice to have someone to talk to, and Art actually seemed to listen to what she had to say. And she listened to him.

It was funny, Camille thought. She had never known her father—he had left before she was born. She had always told people that she didn't think about him, but that was a lie. It was easier to lie rather than admit that it did bother her. Sometimes she sat up at night and wondered why he had left, what he was doing, and why he had never reached out to her. It was not something she could discuss with her mother. Her mother was great, and Camille never wanted her to feel that she had not done enough. But the thoughts about her father never went away, and she had always felt very alone in those thoughts—until she had met Art. Art's mother had died when he was only four years old. Art had told her that he had only the vaguest of memories about her. Camille knew this bothered him, and she also knew that he missed his mom even though he had never really known her. And it meant she wasn't alone. They had both lost parents—albeit under very different circumstances. That was part of their connection. That was part of their friendship.

And so the walk home with Art had become more than just part of her daily routine. It had become a time when she could talk about things—things that mattered to her. Things she couldn't tell anyone else.

And then a week ago, it had all changed. Art had disappeared.

To be clear, he had not *actually* disappeared. He had not been kidnapped or run away. He had not moved. He had not lost his memory and wandered off—again. He still lived in the same house, and she still saw him at school.

But once school was over?

Gone.

Vanished.

For the past week he had simply disappeared as soon as the final school bell rang.

At first she had wondered if she had done something wrong. Had she said something that upset him? Camille knew she had a way of just saying whatever came to her mind. It was one of her less dazzling qualities, and it had made it difficult at times to make friends at school. But Art had never seemed embarrassed about being seen with her. And, try as she might, she couldn't think of anything she might have said or done that would have upset him. Besides, he had a pretty thick skin.

She eliminated a whole host of other possibilities. He clearly wasn't sick—she would still see him occasionally in the hallway at school. He wasn't involved in an after-school project or on one of the sports teams—she had searched the school and the gym the previous day but hadn't seen any sign of him. And he definitely wasn't heading home after school—she would have seen him somewhere along the short route.

That left only one real possibility—a possibility that made her stomach ache: Art had clearly found some new friends. To be fair, she knew that this might eventually happen. Even though Art could be a little strange at times, he was still pretty cool. When he had first started at her school, Camille had known it wouldn't take long for some of the other students to figure that out. And, once it happened, she knew she would find herself walking home alone —again. It had seemed as though it was an inevitability. She kept telling herself that it was okay—it was good for Art to make other friends. He was, after all, a year older than she was. He couldn't be expected to hang out with her forever.

But, still, it hurt.

She had thought about simply grabbing him in the hallway during school and asking him what was going on. But she couldn't. Every time she had seen him at school over the past week, the words just got stuck in her throat. Besides, what was she going to do? Accuse him of making friends?

After a week of standing alone in the courtyard after school, she had decided to find out what was going on once and for all, confirm what she thought she knew. And if she couldn't find the courage to actually speak to him directly about it, she would do the next best thing—follow him after school. It was, she conceded, a bit creepy. But she needed to know. She had told her mom that she was going to hang out with Art after school and that she would be home a little later than usual. It was only a little white lie, she told herself.

And so, ten minutes before the end of the final period of the school day, Camille had asked her teacher for permission to go to the library to pick up a book she had left there. She had not actually lied to her teacher. She had left the book in the library on purpose—carefully hidden behind one of the computers. The library was just a short walk from the hallway in which Art's final class was located. As soon as the final bell of the day rang, Camille had sprinted down the hallway and positioned herself so that she could get a clear view of Art's classroom. Seconds later, she spotted him. He had his backpack over his shoulder, and he was moving quickly in the opposite direction. She followed him at a safe distance as he made his way through the school and, eventually, to the rear entrance. She watched as he pushed the door open and, without as much as a glance backwards, headed straight out toward the street. Camille had hurried up to the window at the rear entrance and watched as Art made his way along M Street.

And—she had noted—he was heading east.

A broad smile had crossed Camille's face.

Although they normally exited through the front of the school, she had actually accompanied Art through the rear entrance on a handful of occasions after school. And each time they had done so, they had headed in the same direction in which Art was now traveling.

So, Camille had thought, *it isn't a new friend.*

She felt somewhat ashamed at how jealous she had been over the possibility that Art may have found someone else to hang out with after school. She knew it was petty and selfish—but she also felt a great deal of relief. Art was not just a friend—he was her best friend.

But this turn of events still left one question unanswered—why was Art going to the Portrait Gallery by himself? He had never hesitated to invite her along in the past. Art was by nature a teacher. He enjoyed walking through the Portrait Gallery with her, pointing out works of art and telling her about the artists. He wasn't the least bit conceited or condescending when he did this—he just wanted to share what he knew, as if the information had been building up inside of him, just waiting to get out.

So why, Camille wondered, would Art head off to the gallery by himself without mentioning anything to her? It was a mystery, and a mystery that Camille determined could be solved only in one way: by following Art. And it was the decision to follow Art that had led Camille to her current situation—standing alone in the lobby of the Portrait Gallery.

"Are you looking for the boy?"

The voice caught Camille by surprise.

She turned to find an older man standing directly behind her. He was dressed in the dark blue uniform worn by the security guards at the Portrait Gallery. He had gray hair and an equally gray mustache. He looked down at her over a pair of round glasses that perched precariously on the end of his narrow nose.

"Excuse me?" Camille asked.

"I asked if you were looking for the boy?" the man said. "You know, Arthur."

Arthur?

The use of Art's full name caught her off-guard for a moment, but she recovered quickly.

"Yes," she said, "I'm looking for Art—I mean, Arthur. His dad is the director of the Lunder Center."

The guard smiled and extended his hand. "My name is Phillip," he said. "But my friends call me Phil. I thought I had seen the two of you here together. I've grown quite fond of Arthur and his father. They practically live here, you know. I bet I see the boy three or four times a week—maybe more."

Camille took the guard's hand and shook it. "Camille Sullivan," she said. "Did you happen to see which way he went?"

She had waited until Art had entered the building before following him. The problem was that once he entered the building, there were any number of directions in which he could have gone. The lobby gave way to long corridors to the east and the west as well as a large interior courtyard. And a set of stairs and an elevator immediately adjacent to the lobby provided access to both the basement below as well as the two floors above. On top of all that, each floor contained a maze of small galleries. Art could be anywhere in the building by now—and it was a very big building.

"Of course," the security guard replied. "He got here not too long ago—you barely missed him. Such a polite young man. Yes sir, always stops and says hello. Not many kids do that nowadays, you know—they just pass on by like I'm not even standing there. But not Arthur. His dad raised him right. Are you one of his classmates? Or maybe you're related?"

Camille didn't want to be impolite, but she really didn't have time for a long conversation about how polite Arthur—Art—was.

"We go to the same school," she replied. "He . . . uh . . . left something behind, and I just wanted to get it to him as soon as possible. I don't want him to worry about it."

The older gentleman started nodding. "Of course, of course," he said. "Well, that makes you quite the good friend. I'll tell you, back in the day I had a friend just like you. His name was Patrick, but we all called him Tadpole. You see, his dad was called Frog."

The security guard paused. "I never knew what his dad's real name was," he finally said. "I don't suppose it was really Frog, but I guess you never know. I also once knew a guy named Newt, so maybe my friend's dad really was named Frog."

"Um, Phillip?" Camille asked. "Did you happen to see which way he headed?"

"My goodness," the security guard replied. "Here I am, running off at the mouth again. I do that sometimes. I think you'll find him in the Great Hall—that's where he's been lurking about the past few days."

Lurking?

"And the Great Hall is . . . ?" Camille asked.

She was still learning her way around the National Portrait Gallery.

Phil pointed toward a set of double doors on the far side of the lobby. "Directly across the courtyard, into the south wing, and then take the stairs to the third floor," he said.

"Oh," said Camille, "*that* room. The big room."

"Yes," the security guard replied with a smile, "*that* room."

Camille turned to head across the courtyard. "Thank you, Phillip."

The security guard gave her a wink. "Remember, it's Phil to my friends," he said. "And you are quite welcome, Camille. Stop by anytime and say hello!"

CHAPTER 6

4:32 p.m.

Friday, April 15

National Portrait Gallery, Washington, DC

From his vantage point on the west end of the third-floor mezzanine, he had a clear view down the length of the Great Hall. Art stood in the corner next to a massive canvas of a boxing match painted in 1944 by the artist James Montgomery Flagg—the same painter who had painted the iconic portrait of Uncle Sam during World War I. The painting near Art was almost twenty feet long and more than five feet tall. It portrayed boxer Jack Dempsey in the midst of his championship bout with Jess Willard—Dempsey and Willard were engaged in the middle of the ring while the crowd around them roared.

The particular section of the mezzanine in which the

painting was hanging was known as the Champions exhibit—a showcase of canvases of some of the most famous and influential sports figures in American history. But despite the magnificent portraits on the wall, the most spectacular part of the Great Hall was the room itself.

Art believed the Great Hall was the most beautiful room in the entire city of Washington, DC. The hall was divided into two wings that swept out to the east and west from the landing at the top of the stairs leading to the third floor of the Portrait Gallery. The floor of the hall was a vast tile mosaic—a repeating pattern of geometric shapes in blue, white, burnt orange, and yellow. The ceiling—rising more than two stories in the air—was glass, and natural light flowed through and across the vast open space. A mezzanine encircled each wing and divided the space into an upper and lower gallery. The Great Hall wasn't just a room that held art—it *was* art.

The building in which the National Portrait Gallery was located had once served as the United States Patent Office—the place where inventors would go to get official recognition of their ideas. That recognition—or proof of the invention—was a piece of paper called a patent. The Great Hall had once served as a vast exhibition space for models of all of the inventions that had been the subjects of those patents. People would come from all over the world to see the models. But now, as the name of the building suggested, the room was filled with portraits—portraits of famous athletes, entertainers, politicians, artists, authors, and other celebrities.

But Art was not there to admire the architecture or the art. He was not there for a history lesson.

He was waiting for someone.

He checked his watch.

It was now 4:34 p.m.

Two minutes to go.

Art turned his attention back to the Great Hall—and that's when he saw her. But it wasn't the "her" he was expecting.

No, no, no, no.

Art couldn't believe what he was seeing.

Standing in the middle of the Great Hall was Camille.

What is she doing here?

Art knew immediately that he didn't have time to consider why or how Camille had suddenly appeared at the Portrait Gallery. Those were questions to be answered at a later time. The only thing he could do right now was to keep her from ruining all the work he had done over the past week.

For a moment he considered simply staying in place.

Maybe she won't see me, he thought.

But Art knew in an instant that this strategy would fail —and fail spectacularly. After all, it wasn't as if he were actually hidden from view—he was standing in a corner at the far end of the hall.

Inconspicuous? Yes—and that was exactly his plan.

But hidden? Not at all.

And if Camille spotted him (and she would), she would immediately start calling his name, waving her arms, or doing something to get his attention. Everybody in the Great Hall would immediately know where he was, and that wasn't a chance he could take. That left only one option.

Art glanced down at his watch.

One and a half minutes to go.

He needed to hurry.

To avoid being spotted from below, Art bent down underneath the ornate cast-iron railing that encircled the mezzanine and carefully made his way toward the center of the hall. He passed beneath portraits of Arthur Ashe, Larry Bird, Muhammad Ali, and Mia Hamm.

"Where are his parents?" he heard one museum patron whisper to another, the annoyance clear in the man's voice.

Art ignored the comment. They didn't know what was going on. They didn't understand the consequences.

Finally, he arrived at the narrow staircase leading down to the main level of the Great Hall. Art slipped down to the landing in the middle of the stairs and took a quick peek over the edge of the railing. Camille was facing in the opposite direction—toward the east wing of the Great Hall—but she was now fewer than twenty feet away from where he was hidden. He pulled out his phone and quickly started typing.

CHAPTER 7

4:35 p.m.

Friday, April 15

National Portrait Gallery, Washington, DC

Where is he?

The security guard had seemed certain that Art would be in the Great Hall—and Camille had little reason to doubt what she had been told. The problem was that the Great Hall was massive—two long wings with multiple galleries that branched off from each wing. Her initial strategy had been to stand in the middle of the hall and perhaps catch sight of Art moving about from one gallery in the hall to the next. But that strategy had not proved particularly successful, and Camille had little patience for simply standing in place hoping that something would happen. To her right—toward the east wing of the museum—was a series of galleries with portraits of twentieth-century Americans. It seemed as good a place to start as any.

Camille had taken precisely one step toward the east wing when a buzzing sound in her backpack brought her to a halt.

She had received a text message.

The backpack buzzed again. And then once more. Three in succession.

Uh-oh, Camille thought. Her heart jumped in her chest.

After the incident at the National Gallery back in December, Camille's mother had finally decided that Camille needed a phone. That was the good news—she could now call her friends (actually, it was mostly Art she called), watch videos, and post pictures of her cat, Ms. Fluffers, on Instagram. However, the phone also came with a condition—that whenever her mom called or texted, she was supposed to respond immediately, or else.

I'm busted, Camille thought.

Has my mother figured out what I've done?

Camille put down her backpack, took a deep breath, and retrieved her phone. To her surprise and to her great relief, the messages were not from her mother.

"Don't look around and don't say anything," the first message read.

Well, that was strange.

It took every bit of self-control she had not to look around.

Calm down, she told herself.

She checked the next message.

"Turn around, go to the metal stairs on the right side of the hall, and go up," the second message read.

Camille glanced around. She could see the stairs, but there was no sign of Art.

She checked the final message.

"And DON'T SAY ANYTHING," the final message read. An unnecessary use of capital letters, in Camille's opinion. There was no need to yell.

Camille put her phone back into her backpack, threw it over her shoulder, and—acting as naturally as possible—made her way to the metal stairs on the right side of the hall and started climbing.

He could hear the soft pad of her shoes on the steps as she made her way up the first flight of stairs to the small landing. Art now sat at the top of the stairs directly above the landing. He was shielded from Camille's view by the thick metal railing of the stairs. He checked his watch—he now had less than a minute.

A moment later Camille appeared on the landing, her bright red hair flying in all directions. It took Camille a second to realize Art was sitting there—and he could see words starting to form on her lips. He motioned for her to be quiet and then pointed at the empty space on the stairs beside him. Camille frowned but kept her words to herself and made her way up the final set of stairs to sit down beside him.

"Thirty seconds," he whispered in her ear, and pointed at the hallway down below.

A look of confusion appeared on Camille's face, but there was no time for an explanation.

CHAPTER 8

4:36 p.m.

Friday, April 15

National Portrait Gallery, Washington, DC

Art stared in silence at the floor below in the Great Hall. Camille glanced over his shoulder hoping to discover the object of his attention but saw nothing out of the ordinary.

Moments later, Art whispered again. "C'mon," he said, "we need to get going."

"Going where?" she whispered back.

"No time to explain," Art replied as he started down the stairs.

Camille shrugged and followed. This wasn't the weirdest situation she had encountered with Art. And at least this time no one was trying to kill them—at least not yet.

Art reached the bottom of the stairs and peeked into the hall. He nodded his head. "Yes, yes," he muttered to himself, and then checked the time on his phone.

He turned to Camille.

"It's 4:36," he said, as if she completely understood the significance of the statement.

As she had done at the top of the stairs, Camille once

more peeked over Art's shoulder in the direction he had been looking. But as before, the object of Art's focus remained lost to her.

Before she could ask for an explanation, Art started making his way across the Great Hall toward the main stairs that led to the floors below. Camille scrambled to catch up. Art navigated the stairs quickly, his long legs covering two steps at a time. Camille did her best to stay close. Moments later they arrived in the lobby on the main floor. Art turned under the stairs toward a set of glass doors facing toward the middle of the building—a large open courtyard. He stopped and checked the time. He then turned his attention to the courtyard itself.

Camille made her way over and glanced around Art into the courtyard. It was her favorite part of the museum—a massive open space filled with green plants, flowers, and trees. It was covered by a wavy canopy of glass and steel that exposed the entire room to the sunlit sky above. The latticelike canopy—four stories above the ground—cast a checkerboard pattern of light and shadows across the far wall. A coffee shop sat in the far right corner surrounded by small tables at which museum patrons consumed lattes and munched on scones. Camille glanced around the familiar space for any sign of what was causing Art to act so strangely. But everything appeared normal.

"What's going on?" Camille whispered.

"Two," Art said, once more offering no explanation.

Art opened the glass doors, and they slipped inside the courtyard. He pointed to their right—to a wide marble bench encircling a long raised bed filled with plants. They made their way to the far side of the raised bed and took a seat on the bench. Art checked the time on his phone again.

"One and a half minutes," he said, then turned his attention to the far side of the courtyard. Camille—once more—gazed in the same direction, and the object of Art's attention—once more—eluded her. People meandered slowly across the courtyard. They sat on the benches and at tables—some alone, some in small groups. A maintenance man dressed in green emptied a trash can in the far corner of the courtyard. Nothing about the scene struck her as out of the ordinary. And yet, this same scene—as mundane and normal as it appeared to her—had become the sole focus of her friend's attention. Art almost seemed to be holding his breath waiting for something. But what?

They had been sitting on the bench for almost a minute, and Camille started to slowly count down from sixty. When her internal clock hit zero, she once again assessed the scene in front of her. Nothing appeared to have changed. Nothing seemed out of the ordinary.

It was time for answers.

"What's going on?" Camille whispered. "Why are you sneaking around like this?"

Art turned and looked at her. "You won't believe me. Nobody will believe me—at least not yet."

"What do you mean by that?" Camille asked. "All I know is that you've been leaving right after school and avoiding me for the entire week. I'm your friend—or maybe you forgot? I'll believe you."

Art could feel the blood rushing to his face. He felt ashamed for avoiding Camille and not telling her what had been going on. But everything had happened so quickly. He had thought it would be best to keep everything to himself until he had more proof. And even though he was completely convinced about what was going to happen, the main thing he was missing was exactly that—proof. Perhaps it was time to let someone else know what was about to take place.

Art paused and took a deep breath. This was the first time he had actually said this to another person—and he hoped it didn't sound completely crazy.

"Someone's planning to steal the paintings from the Millennium Exhibit," he said. "And unless they're stopped, a billion dollars' worth of art will disappear forever."

CHAPTER 9

4:40 p.m.

Friday, April 15

National Portrait Gallery, Washington, DC

Art would not allow the conversation to continue until they had left the museum. Camille had texted her mom on the way out the door to let her know that she was walking home with Art. Her mother had offered to pick them up —an offer quickly declined by Camille. It would be a long walk home, but she needed the time alone with Art.

They made their way from the museum and headed west along G Street. It was late in the day, and the sun barely hung on over the buildings in the distance. Camille waited at least half a block before she could not contain herself anymore.

"Who's going to rob the museum?" she asked. It seemed like a reasonable place to start the conversation.

"I'm not completely sure," Art replied. "There's a lady —that's who I was following back at the museum when you showed up. I know she's involved, but I haven't figured out who else."

Camille paused briefly to let Art's words sink in.

She had known Art for only a few months, but they had grown close over that time. Sometimes he acted more like a grownup than a twelve-year-old. He could be extremely serious, particularly when it came to school or talking about art. On other occasions he seemed just like any other kid his age—laughing and joking as they played video games or watched television. But the one thing he had always been was honest. If Art told you something, he really believed it. And if he said that someone was planning to rob the National Portrait Gallery, he really believed it. The question was, why?

"So this lady," Camille said, "she's part of some sort of . . . conspiracy to rob the museum?"

Art nodded. "Yes."

"Did you overhear her say something?" Camille asked. She had an image of the lady discussing her plans in some dark alley with her accomplice—the image of a tall man with a thin mustache and a beret immediately came to mind. There was also a light fog drifting about their feet—just to complete the entire image.

"No," Art replied.

"Did you see her plans?" Camille asked. She now envisioned the lady unrolling and examining a set of plans—a diagram of the museum with detailed notes of how the caper would be pulled off.

"No," he replied.

"Then she's a famous art thief, and you recognized her?"

Art knew all about art, so maybe he also knew all the famous art thieves. Or maybe art museums had Wanted posters with pictures of all the thieves, and he had matched her face?

"No," Art replied.

"Okay," Camille replied. "I give up. Then how do you know she's going to rob the museum?"

"It was the mocha," Art said, "and the forty-two steps."

Camille took a couple of strides down the sidewalk as her brain processed Art's response.

The mocha?

The forty-two steps?

Camille came to a complete and sudden stop.

Art stopped and turned to her. She halfway expected him to break out into a broad smile and tell her he was only kidding. But he didn't. He wasn't smiling, and his eyes conveyed the seriousness of the situation as he clearly saw it.

"The mocha," he repeated, "and the forty-two steps."

CHAPTER 10

4:50 p.m.

Friday, April 15

Washington, DC

They stood in the middle of the sidewalk on G Street. Pedestrians streamed around them, but Camille did not seem inclined to move.

"Mocha?" she asked. "And forty-two steps? What the heck is that supposed to mean?"

It was a fair question. Art had been so caught up in the events of the past week that he had clearly not thought about how crazy his response must have sounded to Camille—or to anyone, for that matter. His decision not to discuss this with his father seemed more than validated by Camille's reaction.

"It does sound a little strange," he said.

"A little?"

"Okay," Art conceded. "A lot strange."

Camille nodded. "Better."

She then pointed down the sidewalk. "We need to get home. So start walking and start talking."

It had all made sense in his head—all of the reasons

why he believed the museum was going to be robbed. But now, faced with the prospect of actually having to explain to someone what he had been doing for the past week, he felt nervous and uncertain. Art took a deep breath and told himself to focus.

"It started with the mocha," Art said. "Last Saturday afternoon I was at the museum with Dad and went down to the café to get a mocha. I was heading back across the courtyard to Dad's office and wasn't paying attention. I ran smack into this lady in the middle of the courtyard—spilled the mocha all over myself and all over the lady's shoes."

"Iced mocha or hot?" Camille asked.

"Iced, of course," replied Art.

"Carry on."

"I really thought she would be furious," said Art. "Her shoes looked expensive, and they were covered with iced mocha. But she didn't get mad at all. I kept trying to apologize, but she told me that she hadn't been paying attention. I ran back to the café and grabbed a bunch of napkins. She actually helped me clean up the mess, if you can believe it."

"Obviously a thief," Camille said as they turned right and headed north on Fourteenth Street.

"Do you want to hear the rest of the story or not?" Art asked.

"Sorry," Camille replied.

"Anyway," Art continued, "I didn't think anything about it—I went back to get something else to drink. I was heading back to my dad's office when I saw her again—she was walking across the courtyard in the same direction that she had been walking when we collided."

"And that's strange because . . . ?" Camille asked.

"Because instead of simply continuing across the courtyard after we crashed," Art explained, "she actually returned to wherever she had started and then started all over again."

"That's a little weird," Camille said, "but that doesn't mean she's a thief."

"Agreed," Art said. "But there's more—there was also the way she was walking."

Art paused. This was the crucial point in the story—he needed to get it right.

"Have you ever watched a marching band?" he asked.

"Of course," Camille replied. "I've been to a ton of parades—there're always marching bands in a parade."

"The woman at the museum walked sort of like someone in a marching band," Art explained. "Every step she took was exactly the same—the same distance between each and every step. It looked like she was marching."

"Again," Camille said, "maybe a little weird, but so what?"

"So nothing," Art replied. "It was just something I noticed. I didn't even think anything else about it. Trust me, I've seen a lot weirder stuff than that at museums. But then the next day I was in the courtyard doing my homework."

"And you saw her again?" Camille said.

"Yep," he replied. "At the exact same time as Saturday—at exactly 4:30 in the afternoon. And she was walking exactly like she had been on Saturday. Not *sorta* the same—*exactly* the same. Straight across the courtyard—each step exactly the same."

"It could be just a coincidence," Camille said. "And maybe she was in the army or something—they march, don't they? And there're all sorts of reasons she might have come back to the museum—that doesn't mean she's a thief."

Art nodded. "No. It doesn't mean she's a thief."

Art could feel himself starting to get frustrated. He told himself to calm down. He knew this wasn't going to be easy. Camille was his friend—and her questions were fair, even if they stung a little. Besides, Camille trusted him. And if he couldn't convince Camille, whom could he convince?

CHAPTER 11

4:53 p.m.

Friday, April 15

Washington, DC

The sun now sat on the top of a stone building in the distance—the clouds glowed a bright orange as the last of the day lingered in the sky. The shadows along the street had grown long and deep. They were nearing home, and Camille felt no closer to understanding Art's certainty that the National Portrait Gallery was going to be robbed. But Art was her friend, and she was willing to give him the benefit of the doubt—no matter how crazy it sounded.

"So what about the forty-two steps?" she asked.

"I know it sounds stupid, but I couldn't get the lady out of my mind," Art said. "So I went back to the museum after school on Monday to see if she came back."

"And she did," Camille said.

"At the exact same time as she had been there on Saturday and Sunday," he replied. "Not sorta the same time—the exact same time. And that's when I started counting. She took exactly forty-two steps to cross the courtyard—every step exactly the same as Saturday and Sunday."

"Maybe it just looked the same," Camille said. "Maybe it was forty-one steps on Sunday, or forty-three steps on Saturday. How could you know?"

"I also thought of that," Art said. "I mean, how could she have taken the exact same number of steps on all three days? So I went back to the museum on Tuesday—and so did she. She showed up at exactly 4:30 p.m. And do you want to guess how many steps she took to get across the courtyard?"

"Forty-two," Camille replied.

"Exactly," Art said. "That can't be a coincidence."

"So is that it?" Camille asked. "Is that why you think she's going to rob the museum? It's weird, but . . . you know . . . I'm not sure that's enough to prove she's part of some conspiracy to steal all those paintings."

Art nodded. "You're right. It's not enough. But I knew something was up—I just didn't know what. So on Wednesday I followed her out of the courtyard and into the museum."

"That's sorta creepy, you know," Camille said.

"And following your friend after school isn't?" Art asked.

"Fair enough," she replied. "You may continue."

"I had to know what she was doing," Art said, "and that's when it got even weirder. The lady kept walking, and she never stopped."

That's it? Camille thought. *She kept walking?*

"She went right out of the courtyard," Art continued,

"up the stairs to the second floor, around the entire floor, then up the stairs to the third floor, around that entire third floor. I almost lost her when she got back to the stairs on the third floor—I wasn't sure where she was going. But I looked out the window that faces out to the courtyard and there she was."

"Where?" Camille asked.

"She took the stairs right back down to the courtyard," Art replied, "and headed back out the same way she'd come in. I checked my phone—it took her exactly eight minutes and thirty seconds."

"Maybe she's just getting her steps in," Camille said. "Some people are like that, you know. My mom obsesses over getting ten thousand steps every day. She's constantly checking the monitor on her watch. Sometimes she'll pace back and forth in the living room just to make sure she gets enough steps in before she goes to bed—and I'm pretty sure my mom isn't an art thief."

The last comment came out with a bit more sarcasm that she had intended. She glanced over at Art, but he didn't seem upset—he seemed lost in the story he was telling.

"And then there was today," Art said. "She showed up at the exact same time as she always does and she walked the exact same route as yesterday. I don't mean sorta the same—I mean exactly, precisely, and completely the same. Forty-two steps across the courtyard and eight minutes and thirty seconds from start to finish."

Okay, Camille finally had to concede to herself, *that is starting to get a little weird.*

But it still didn't mean the lady was an art thief. There were still other possible explanations. Camille was convinced that there had to be more to the story than what Art had already told her.

"I'm not trying to be mean, but I don't think anyone's going to believe you," Camille said. "Forty-two steps and an iced mocha . . . Well, that's not really going to make sense to anyone, is it?"

Art shook his head. "No," he replied. "It isn't, but there's more."

They had now reached the end of the block where they both lived. Art stopped and turned to Camille.

"I've spent my life in museums," he said. "They're the closest thing that I've ever had to a real home—until now. It's hard to describe, but there's a rhythm to a museum. It's the way people act when they go to an art museum. The way they walk. The way they look at the art. The way they talk to one another. It's the way the docents and the security guards make their way from room to room. It's the tour groups. It's the artists setting up their easels to copy an old master painting. It's the sounds, the smells, and the lights. And when you've been in museums as much I have, you just know when something's not right.

"This lady," he continued, "she doesn't fit the rhythm—and that's what bothers me. She's not a tourist—that's for sure. She's not dressed like a tourist, and she sure doesn't act like a tourist. She's wearing heels, not walking shoes. She doesn't stop to look at the art. She doesn't carry around a map of the museum trying to figure out how to get around. She doesn't ask questions or read any of the descriptions on the paintings. She doesn't carry a purse, a briefcase, or a backpack. She has a phone, but she never uses it. But every day for the past week she has been coming back to the museum for some reason—and it isn't to see the paintings hanging on the walls."

Art paused. "I know that probably doesn't make sense to you," he finally said, "but it makes all the sense in the world to me. She's up to something—and I think it has something to do with the Millennium Exhibit."

Camille wasn't convinced the lady was a thief, but what Art was feeling did make sense.

"Last summer," she said, "I went off to camp for two weeks. When I got home, I walked inside and had this weird feeling that something was different about my house. I didn't want to ask my mom because it sounded so stupid. Everything seemed exactly the same—but I just had this feeling. It drove me crazy for an entire week. Something just seemed off, so I finally asked my mom."

"What was it?" Art asked.

"Mom had switched two of the chairs in the living room," Camille replied. "That was it—just a little change. Same chairs, different places."

Art nodded. "But you knew something was off," he said, "even though you didn't know exactly what it was."

"Yep," Camille replied. "I just felt it."

They walked along in silence for half a block until they stood at the bottom of the steps leading up to Camille's front door. It had grown dark, and the warm day had given way to an exceedingly cool evening—a reminder that spring had yet to officially arrive.

"It's going to be tough to prove," Camille said. "You're going to need more than a mocha and forty-two steps if anyone is going to believe you."

Art sighed. "I know."

"Then I guess we better get started tomorrow," Camille replied.

Art watched as Camille made her way up the steps to the front door, where she was greeted by her mother. Mary Sullivan invited Art in for dinner, but he politely declined. He made his way toward the end of the block—toward the narrow three-story house that he now called home. His father would be off work soon, and they were planning to go out for pizza.

It had been difficult, but Art felt relieved after telling Camille the secret he had been harboring for the past week.

He knew he should have told her sooner, and he regretted the worry that he had caused her. He should have trusted her sooner. He knew she would always be honest with him.

The conversation with Camille had caused him to reexamine his own conclusions. Was it possible he could be wrong? Could there be other plausible explanations for what the woman was doing at the museum? And although he remained convinced that the woman was part of a plot to steal some of the most famous paintings in the world, he could not allow himself to get so caught up in his own theories that he lost all perspective. Their mission was not to prove that a theft was being planned, not to fit the facts to his own conclusion—their mission was to uncover the truth.

CHAPTER 12

6:33 p.m.

Friday, April 15

Hotel Montgomery, Washington, DC

The Hotel Montgomery sat just off Pennsylvania Avenue a few blocks north of the White House. The Monty—as it was known by locals—first opened its doors in 1919. The hotel remained remarkably similar in appearance and operation to the day of its grand opening more than a century past—thick stone walls, rich wood panels, polished brass fixtures, and a thoughtful and attentive staff. It was small by modern standards—and proudly so. The lobby of the hotel was barely large enough to accommodate a handful of guests, the hallways were narrow, and the hotel boasted only thirty rooms over the course of its four floors. The hotel did not have any of the amenities expected of today's hotels. There was no conference center, no grand ballroom, no exercise room, and no business center. And yet the hotel was among the most popular in the city—and for good reason. The concierge had an unparalleled knowledge of the city (and the uncanny ability to secure a seat at any restaurant or a ticket to any event in DC). The small restaurant that sat at the front of the building offered the finest steaks in town. The rooms were luxurious. And, above all, there was the Archive Room.

The Archive Room was located at the rear of the building on the second floor. It sat at the end of a long, narrow hallway just past the elevator. It was a restaurant, of sorts. It was not advertised to the public and did not accept reservations. The menu was limited—little more than sandwiches and drinks. There were no exterior windows, and the room was surrounded on three sides by two feet of stone exterior wall. It was disarmingly dark inside—the dark blue wallpaper and mahogany molding seemed to absorb any light in the room—and each table was partially shrouded by a heavy canopy that dropped from the ceiling. Time seemed to stand still in the Archive Room. There were no external clues as to the time of day or weather, and the room lacked any hint of modernity. The only sound was a low murmur of conversation that seemed to pervade the room at all times.

Presidents, ambassadors, kings, politicians, spies, and diplomats have sat at the small tables of the Archive Room for generations and discussed whatever such people discuss when they are alone. Guests seeking the solitude and quiet of the room were greeted at the door by the maitre d' —a large, dark-haired man who introduced himself simply as Robert. Robert greeted all guests the same—never by name, and never with any sense that they have been to the room on a prior occasion. No one was remembered in the

Archive Room, and yet no one was ever quite forgotten. Above all else, the Archive Room, its staff, and its guests valued discretion—and it was that discretion that led Catherine Dismuke to the Monty on this particular spring day.

Dismuke exited the elevator and stepped into the small hallway on the second floor of the Hotel Montgomery.

"Good evening," Robert said as she approached the entrance. Painted above the door in a flowing script was the word *Archive.* The maitre d's tone was pleasant and professional—but it did not escape Dismuke's attention that Robert was roughly the size of a tank. His muscular frame filled the entire doorway. Security, it appeared, was not an issue.

"I'm meeting a client this afternoon," Dismuke said. "I was hoping a table might be available." She could see into the interior of the room, but it was impossible to tell if anyone was actually seated at any of the canopy-draped tables.

"Your client has already arrived," Robert replied.

Dismuke simply nodded. She did not bother to ask how Robert knew who she was or with whom she was meeting. She had been told that the less she asked, the better. The Archive Room and its guests preferred it that way.

Robert held out a small wicker basket filled with cell phones. "Your cell phone, please," he said. The tone of his voice was polite but firm.

Dismuke dropped her cell phone into the basket.

"This way," Robert said. He motioned for Dismuke to follow him into the dark interior of the chamber.

As they wound their way through the room, Dismuke caught brief glimpses of shadowy figures sitting at several of the tables. There was a low murmur of indistinct conversation throughout the room. She reminded herself to keep her eyes forward—their business was not her business, and her business was not their business.

Finally, Robert came to a stop at a small table near the rear of the room—although, to be honest, Dismuke could not be certain as to exactly where in the room she was now standing.

Robert pulled back the canopy. "Enjoy your evening," he said.

Dismuke stepped inside, and the canopy was drawn behind her.

"You're early," Dismuke said as she took her seat at the small round table.

"I'm always early," the man sitting across from her replied. "I assume the project is proceeding as planned?"

Her client was not a man given over to useless chatter or small talk.

"The project is going as planned," Dismuke said. "Do you want the details?"

"No," the man replied. "I hired you to handle the details."

He paused and took a sip of water. "How much longer?" he finally asked. "Will we be ready?"

"Everything will be ready by tomorrow," Dismuke assured him. "One last visit to the museum—that's all I need."

The man nodded. "Very well."

And with that, their conversation was over. The man stood and—without another word—pulled back the canopy and departed. Dismuke relaxed in her seat. It had been a long but productive week. Although there were still details to work out and refine, she already knew exactly what she would do and how she would do it. This job may have been the biggest she had ever undertaken, but she had spent most of her adult life developing the experience and knowledge necessary to carry out the task. And even though her assignment involved a billion dollars' worth of paintings from the National Portrait Gallery, she was ready.

CHAPTER 13

10:30 a.m.
Saturday, April 16
The Bean and Bread, Washington, DC

The smell of coffee and freshly baked pastries filled the air in the small café. The Saturday morning crowd had settled comfortably into their seats, their iPads and laptops propped in front of them, their headphones and ear buds in place, and their lattes and cappuccinos at the ready. Camille ran her finger across the small plate in front of her to capture the last few crumbs of her *butterkuchen,* an almond pastry filled with cream. It was the café's most popular pastry—a designation that Camille felt was more than warranted. She took a sip of her hot chocolate and then leaned back in her chair. It was time to get to work.

The night before, she had asked her mom if she could spend the day with Art at the National Portrait Gallery—not a particularly surprising request. She had spent a lot of time at the museum since Art's father had taken the job at the Lunder Conservation Center. However, the museum did not open until 11:30, and Art had insisted that they needed to spend some time discussing their plans for the day. Such plans, Camille had replied, were best drawn up with a warm almond pastry and a hot chocolate. But before they could get to any planning, Camille still had one major question that she had not been able to get out of her head since their discussion the previous day.

"You think someone's planning to steal the paintings in the exhibit, right?" she asked.

Art nodded. "That's right."

Camille paused. There was no easy way to say what she had been thinking—so she decided to just say it.

"That just seems . . . well . . . impossible," she said. "I could see, like, one painting getting stolen, but all of them? How would they even get that many paintings out of the museum? And where would they go? Just drive off? The police would catch them before they could even get a block."

Camille's words lingered in the air, and she braced for Art's reaction. Maybe he would be angry with her, although Art was not particularly prone to losing his temper. Maybe he would just get quiet—Art did have a tendency to do that sometimes. Or maybe he would become argumentative. He also had a tendency to do that as well, particularly when he thought he was right. But the truth was that no one could ever get away with stealing that many paintings from a museum without getting caught. The museum was located in the middle of a big city, not some little town in the middle of nowhere. It was impossible—and Art needed to hear someone say that.

To her surprise, Art calmly took a sip of his iced mocha and then sat back in his chair. "It does seem impossible," he conceded. "The idea that thieves could walk into a museum and steal a bunch of famous paintings sounds crazy.

"The problem," he continued, "is that it has happened before—almost exactly thirty years ago."

Camille's jaw dropped open. "Wait," she said. "This has happened before?"

That didn't seem possible. Art had to be exaggerating.

"The Isabella Stewart Gardner Museum," Art said. "It's a private museum in Boston. The lady it's named after built an Italian palace in the middle of the city—four stories tall with an open courtyard in the middle. It's absolutely gorgeous. Mrs. Gardner lived on the top floor of the museum and filled the rest of the building with antique furniture, sculptures, flags, tapestries, and a ton of paintings. And not just any paintings—famous paintings by really famous painters. Trust me, the museum is not like anything you have ever seen."

Art leaned across the table. "Late one night—it was actually St. Patrick's Day—two thieves pretending to be police officers convinced security guards to let them into the museum. They tied up the guards and stole a half billion dollars' worth of art—three Rembrandts, five drawings by Degas, a Manet, a Vermeer and other stuff."

Half a billion dollars' worth of art?

"So what happened?" Camille asked. "They caught them, right?"

Art shook his head. "Nope. They were never caught. The thieves just drove off into the night, and the artwork has never been found."

Camille was stunned. She was certainly not an expert on art, but the names of the artists that Art had just mentioned were well known even to her—Rembrandt, Vermeer, Degas, Manet. It was hard to imagine so much artwork simply vanishing into thin air. She could hear the emotion in Art's voice. She could tell how much this meant to him.

"I told you that Rembrandt painted all sort of portraits," Art said, "including a ton of self-portraits. But in his entire career he painted one seascape—in 1633, when he was only twenty-seven years old. It's a picture of a boat caught in a storm, waves crashing all around it. Most of the painting is dark—the water and the sky look like they are trying to swallow the boat and the passengers. But there is this small opening in the clouds and you can see the blue sky breaking through the darkness. It's incredible."

Art paused for a moment, seemingly lost in his own thoughts. Camille knew he had a tendency to do that when he started talking about art.

"The seascape is one of the paintings that was stolen from the Gardner Museum," Art finally said. "I've seen virtually every Rembrandt painting in every museum on the planet. And that's the one I haven't seen yet in person. It was stolen before I was even born. And it's gone, maybe forever."

"But how could that happen?" Camille asked. The whole story seemed impossible—like a movie. How do two thieves walk away with a half billion dollars' worth of art?

"A lot of people think the thieves had help," Art explained. "Maybe even someone who worked at the museum—an insider. The thieves seemed to know everything about the security at the museum. They knew exactly how many guards would be there and where the video footage was kept. They knew where the silent alarm was located. Most art thefts last less than ten minutes—in and out quickly to avoid getting caught. But the thieves stayed in the museum for eighty-one minutes. The police could never prove that anyone working at the museum had helped the thieves—everyone seemed to have an alibi."

"Eighty-one minutes?" Camille said. "It doesn't sound like they were worried about getting caught."

"No," Art replied. "They weren't worried at all. They knew what they were doing—and they knew exactly what they were looking for. The guys who stole the art didn't just go through each room and steal random paintings. They stole specific works of art. They knew the museum backwards and forward—they knew exactly where everything was. They walked through rooms filled with masterpieces just to get to the art they wanted. It was like they were shopping. They knew what they wanted, and they went and got it. They were professionals, and they pulled off the biggest art theft in history."

Something clicked in Camille's head.

"That's what you think the woman is doing?" Camille said. "Getting to know the museum backwards and forward?"

Art nodded. "Exactly."

"And you think it's going to happen again."

"I do," Art responded. "When you go to the Gardner Museum today, they have empty frames hanging on the wall. Three Rembrandts — gone. A Vermeer — one of only thirty-four in the entire world — gone. Five drawings by Degas — gone. A painting by Manet — gone. All that's left are empty frames to show where the paintings would have been."

Art leaned over the table. "Do you remember the paintings that are going to be in the Millennium Exhibit?"

Camille did remember. There was the self-portrait by Rembrandt, and a painting of the young lady in a red hat — the Vermeer. And Art's father had mentioned others as well, including paintings by Degas and Manet.

Rembrandt, Vermeer, Degas, Manet.

Just like the theft at the Gardner Museum. It was probably a coincidence, but it was enough to send a slight chill up Camille's spine.

Art looked at Camille. "No more empty frames," he said.

Camille slumped back in her seat. All of a sudden the thought of someone stealing the paintings in the Millennium Exhibit didn't seem quite so crazy.

"So what's the plan?" Camille asked.

"I know what the lady does when she's in the museum," Art said, "but we need to know where she goes when she leaves."

"We're going to follow her?" Camille asked excitedly —and, by the way Art winced, she guessed she had also spoken a bit too loudly for his comfort. He glanced around, but all of the headphones and ear buds remained firmly in place. No one seemed to have noticed.

"Yes," he whispered. "We're going to follow her. Remember what you told me yesterday—about no one believing me? You're right. I need more proof. And the only way we're going to get that proof is by following her."

"So what do we do when she gets to wherever she's going?" Camille asked. It seemed like a logical question.

Art sat back in his chair. "I don't know. We'll deal with that when we get there."

Camille paused and took another sip of her hot chocolate. "Okay by me," she finally replied. She didn't mind following Art around the city. But there was still one super major problem.

"What about my mom?" Camille asked. "And your dad?

They're not going to just let us run off through the city, are they?"

"No," Art replied. "They're not. But if the lady follows the same pattern as every other day, then she won't show up until almost closing time and . . ."

"And we'll just tell them we're walking home," Camille replied. "And maybe take a little detour along the way?"

Art nodded. "Exactly. I already told my dad that we may head home at some point before the museum closes. He's got plenty to do to get ready for the grand opening, so he didn't seem to mind."

Art paused for a moment. "You don't have to go, you know," he finally said. "If we get caught, we could get in a lot of trouble. You could just call your mother to come get you."

It was clear that Art did not relish the prospect of misleading his father or her mother. It was a feeling that Camille shared, and she knew that her mother would absolutely freak out if she knew what they were planning to do. But she also knew that Art was determined to find out who this mysterious lady was and what she was doing. And he was going to follow the lady whether she went along or not. Camille was not going to let him do that alone.

Besides, what was the worst that could happen?

CHAPTER 14

11:32 a.m.
Saturday, April 16
National Portrait Gallery, Washington, DC

They arrived at the museum just as it opened and positioned themselves at one of the small tables near the café in the courtyard. But after an hour of watching tourists migrate their way back and forth across the open space, Art had decided that it was a waste of time.

"She'll be here at exactly 4:30 this afternoon," he said. "No earlier and no later. There's no sense in just sitting here."

The absolute certainty in Art's voice troubled Camille.

It was lunchtime, so they grabbed a quick bite to eat in the café before drifting over to the galleries to pass the rest of the afternoon. Camille had come to love the National Portrait Gallery and its collection of art. She particularly loved the Portrait Gallery of the presidents of the United States on the second floor. It was set up in chronological order, from George Washington to Barack Obama —a portrait of each president in the past. But there was one particular item in this section of the museum that was her favorite—a portrait of sorts, but not the same as the paintings hanging on the walls. Near the portrait of Abraham Lincoln was a plaster cast of the president's face made during his lifetime. Art explained that it was called a life mask—wet plaster had been applied to the president's face while he was alive. Once dried and removed, the plaster was then used as a mold to produce the life mask in the museum—a three-dimensional image of exactly what President Lincoln looked like. Camille was fascinated by the life mask. There was something exciting and a bit strange about staring into the face of the president who had guided the United States through the Civil War.

They wandered through the rest of the second floor and eventually made their way up to the third floor—to the Lunder Conservation Center, where Art's father worked. Located on the third and fourth floors in the west wing of the museum, the center had large glass panels that allowed the public to watch as the conservationists went about their work. Four sections of the conservation lab could be seen through the glass panels—the frames conversation studio, the paper conservation lab, the paintings conservation lab, and the objects conservation lab. When she had first heard that Art's father was in charge of the conservation labs, Camille didn't know quite what to expect. What exactly did an art conservation laboratory look like? As it turned out pretty much like every other laboratory she had ever seen—white walls, lots of chemicals, large tables, sinks, a massive ventilation system, microscopes, beakers, and bright lights.

When Art and Camille arrived at the conservation center, the only lab that appeared to be in use was the paintings conservation lab—the part of the lab in which the specialists repaired and cleaned paintings. Through the glass, Camille could see the back of a massive painting that was sitting on a large metal easel. It had been removed from its frame, and a technician was carefully examining the edge of the painting. The technician's long dark hair was pulled behind her head in a tight bun, and she wore a weird set of large eyeglasses that appeared to have magnifying lenses attached to them. Camille had hung around the conservation center long enough to know most of the people who worked there. And despite the odd glasses that covered half her face, Camille knew that the technician who was working on the painting was Linda Nguyen—a graduate student working part-time at the center. It was sort of crazy to think about it, but Linda was actually closer in age to Camille and Art than she was to most of the other conservationists working at the center. That was part of the reason Camille liked Linda so much.

Art explained that Linda was examining one of the paintings that would be included in the Millennium Exhibit. His father had insisted that every painting in the exhibit be examined for damage—no matter how small that damage might be—so that it could be documented and appropriate precautions adopted while the exhibition was taking place.

Art had started to explain the effect of humidity on different types of paint when Linda saw them and—mercifully—waved for them to come inside, thus putting an end to Art's impromptu science lecture. Linda met them at the door and buzzed them into the lab.

"So what are you two up to today?" she asked. "Just hanging out at the museum with us art nerds? If you don't watch out, you might become one of us."

Most of the technicians would get so caught up in their work that they never paid attention to the people watching them on the other side of the glass panels—the technicians and scientists tended to be an exceptionally serious group. But Linda always seemed to find time to wave—particularly at any kids who might be watching her as she worked.

Camille motioned toward Art. "It's too late for him," she said. "He's the king of art nerds. Can you believe that he was just starting to tell me about the effect of humidity on paints?"

Linda's eyes immediately lit up. "Oh," she said excitedly, "and did he tell you about the different minerals that can be found in air vapor? That's so important to understand. I just read this great article about calcite and paintings from the late eighteenth century in Europe."

Camille sighed.

"So what are you working on?" Art asked.

"Come see for yourself," Linda replied. She led them over to the painting she had been examining. Art and

Camille stepped around the easel to face the front of the massive painting.

"That's . . . that's Michelle Obama!" Camille exclaimed. In the painting, the former First Lady—seated and wearing a long flowing dress—stared out at the viewer in front of a robin's-egg blue background. Camille had seen the painting numerous times—it was her favorite painting in the entire museum. And it was huge—six feet tall and five feet across.

Linda Nguyen smiled. "It's a very popular painting."

"There nothing wrong with it, is there?" Camille asked. "I mean, it's practically brand-new."

"Right—Amy Sherald painted it in 2018," Linda replied. "And no, there's nothing wrong with it at all. It's actually in great shape. But I'm going to check every inch just to make sure."

"So it's part of the Millennium Exhibit?" Camille asked.

Linda nodded. "It sure is," she replied. "Pretty cool, huh? It may be new, but it's already one of the most famous portraits in America. In fact, Amy Sherald is the only living artist with a painting in the exhibit—as well one of only two women artists who will be displayed."

Camille stood directly in front of the painting. It was the closest she had ever gotten to it without a crowd of other people all around her. It was incredible. The portrait of Michelle Obama was one of the reasons why Camille liked the National Portrait Gallery so much and why it was so different from most art museums. It wasn't just the painting itself (which she adored), but what it represented. The museum was filled with portraits of women who had shaped and continued to shape the direction of the United States. Portraits of women such as Rosa Parks, Gertrude Stein, Lena Horne, Billie Jean King, Toni Morrison, Denyce Graves, and Helen Keller filled the museum. There was even a massive portrait of all of the women who have served as justices of the United States Supreme Court.

And the fact that the Michelle Obama portrait had also been painted by a woman made it even better. Camille already knew that most of the painters included in the Millennium Exhibit were men. That was why the painting by Amy Sherald was so important, as well as the paintings by Mary Cassatt. Most people thought of Monet or Renoir when they thought of Impressionists, but Camille thought that Mary Cassatt was as good as any of them. If the Millennium Exhibit was supposed to celebrate the greatest portrait painters in history, then women needed to be included. She just wished there were more than two in the exhibit.

Camille glanced over at Art, who was looking down at his watch. Art looked up and nodded. It was time.

"Have you seen my dad?" Art asked Linda.

"He took the lift down to the basement a little while ago," she said. "We're expecting a delivery this afternoon

—some piece of pottery coming in from the Netherlands to be cleaned. He should be back soon."

"'Lift'?" Camille said. "What's that?"

"Just another name for an elevator," Art explained. "The conservation center uses it to get the artwork up here from the basement."

Camille had never really thought about how all the artwork got to the conservation center. The center was always filled with paintings and sculptures that were being cleaned and restored—some of them very expensive and very famous. It made sense that technicians wouldn't simply carry things like that through the middle of the museum.

Art turned back to Linda. "Camille and I are going to head home in just a bit," he said. "I'll text my dad before we leave, but if you see him, will you let him know we're heading out?"

Linda Nguyen gave a thumbs-up. "Of course. Be safe, and stay out of trouble."

CHAPTER 15

4:26 p.m.

Saturday, April 16

National Portrait Gallery, Washington, DC

Art and Camille left the conservation center and made their way over to a set of stairs in the west wing of the museum. Art led the way down to a small landing on the second floor. A large window set in the thick stone walls of the museum faced out over the interior courtyard.

Art checked his phone.

"It's 4:28," he said. "She'll be here in two minutes."

Art pointed toward the window—its wide granite ledge provided a perfect place to sit and observe the courtyard below. "We can wait there and watch," he said.

They looked down over the length of the courtyard. Several dozen people mingled about in the large open space—most making their way back and forth from one side of the museum to the other. The seats outside the café were filled with patrons. A couple of small children ran around the large planter to their right.

Everything seemed perfectly normal.

Art pointed at a large set of double doors on the left side of the courtyard. "That's where she'll come in."

He spoke with absolute confidence. There was not a hint of uncertainty in his voice.

Art checked his phone once more. "Thirty seconds."

Camille's heart started to race—both out of excitement for what might happen *and* out of concern for how Art would react if the woman failed to show up.

"Fifteen seconds," Art said. Yet again, he spoke with absolute certainty.

Camille glanced over at Art. His eyes alternated between the clock on his phone and the double doors in the courtyard. A small knot was starting to form in her stomach. It now seemed crazy to think that at precisely 4:30 p.m. this mysterious woman would suddenly walk through those doors.

"Ten seconds," Art said.

Camille turned her attention back to the doors in the courtyard, thinking about what she would say if the woman didn't appear.

"Five seconds," he said.

Camille's mouth suddenly went dry. She wanted to say something—anything—but for once the words didn't come out.

Two teenagers burst through the doors into the courtyard, but no mystery woman.

Camille held her breath.

She's not going to show up, Camille thought.

And then suddenly, as if on cue, the doors to the courtyard opened.

A tall woman wearing a dark blue business suit stepped into the courtyard. She had short brown hair—cropped close to her head—and wore glasses. Camille glanced down at her phone—it was exactly 4:30 p.m.

Not 4:29 p.m.

Not 4:31 p.m.

Precisely, exactly 4:30 p.m.

Art didn't say a word, yet Camille knew immediately that it was *the* woman.

Art had started counting out loud as soon as the woman had entered the courtyard. "One, two, three, four," he said.

There was a rhythm in his voice that matched the woman's exceptionally precise and even steps as she walked. Camille watched as the woman made her way directly across the courtyard toward the doors on the opposite side. Art was right. She didn't look like a tourist at all. She appeared to be dressed as if she were heading to work in some high-rise office building—a look that struck Camille as unusual for a trip to the museum on a Saturday. And there was clearly a purpose to her walk. She was not simply taking a leisurely stroll. She carried a cell phone in her right hand, but she never glanced at it as she walked. Her gaze was straight ahead and unwavering.

"Twenty-three, twenty-four, twenty-five, twenty-six," Art continued.

It was clear that the woman making her way across the courtyard in the National Portrait Gallery was doing so for a very specific reason.

"Thirty-two, thirty-three, thirty-four, thirty-five," Art continued.

Camille glanced over at Art. She was amazed to discover that he had closed his eyes, and yet his cadence continued to match the woman step for step.

Camille returned her gaze to the woman—she had almost reached the double doors on the far side of the courtyard. By chance a young man happened to be entering the courtyard at the same time. He held the door open as the woman approached.

"Forty," said Art as he continued his count.

"Forty-one."

With one final step, the woman reached the threshold of the door.

"Forty-two."

And then she was gone.

Art opened his eyes and turned to Camille.

"Forty-two steps," she said.

Not forty-three.

Not forty-one.

Exactly, precisely forty-two steps.

Art nodded.

Whatever doubts Camille may have had as to whether the mysterious woman existed vanished in an instant. Of course, none of this proved that the woman Camille had just watched make her way across the courtyard was actually planning to rob the museum. But it was now abundantly clear to Camille that this woman was up to something—exactly what remained a mystery.

CHAPTER 16

4:32 p.m.
Saturday, April 16
National Portrait Gallery, Washington, DC

"Let's go," Art said. "We've got ten minutes to get outside and get ready."

They made their way down the winding staircase to the first floor and then paused briefly at the doorway leading into the courtyard. Art cracked open one of the double doors and glanced around the courtyard for any sign of the woman. It was merely a precaution—he already knew exactly where she would be. By now she would have reached the second floor landing and started her route around the second floor.

"All clear," he announced.

They made their way quickly across the courtyard toward the door from which the woman had first appeared. Art knew that it would take her exactly eight and a half minutes to return to the courtyard and head back out the same way she had entered. Where she went after she left the building was still a mystery, but it was a mystery that he intended to solve this afternoon.

They passed through the doors into the lobby on the north side of the building. Art had already picked a location directly across the street from the north entrance to wait for the woman to exit—a point from which they could discreetly observe her leaving the building and then follow her at a safe distance. Art could feel his heart beating furiously in his chest, and all his nerves seemed to be on high alert.

"Don't forget to text your dad that we're leaving," Camille said.

"Thanks," he replied. He had almost forgotten. Fortunately, they still had plenty of time to get outside and position themselves across the street. He stopped in the lobby and typed out a quick message to his father. Art returned the phone to his pocket and had turned once more to leave when a voice suddenly rang out from across the lobby.

"Arthur! Camille!" a man's voice cried out.

They both turned in unison to see Phil the security guard smiling and waving at them from across the foyer. A moment later he was slowly moving in their direction.

"Oh no," Art whispered to Camille.

"'Oh no' what?" Camille asked. "I like Phil."

"So do I," Art said. "He's a really great guy—but he'll talk forever, and we don't have forever."

"Oh, right," Camille replied.

Art glanced down at his phone. They now had fewer than five minutes to make it across the street, and they didn't have time to waste talking with Phil. But Art also knew that he could not risk being rude to the older gentleman. Phil was friends with everyone at the museum—Art's father included. If Art and Camille were rude or seemed to be in a hurry, that news could make its way back to his father.

"Hey, Phil!" Art said as the older gentleman finally made his way over to where they were standing.

"What's up, Phil?" Camille chimed in.

"So what are you kids up to this afternoon?" the security guard asked. "It's a beautiful day outside today—the temperature is absolutely perfect. Not too hot, not too cold—just the way I like it. Hope you have something fun planned. It would be a shame to waste all this great weather."

"No plans," Art replied. "Just hanging out at the museum—we were about to head home."

Phil nodded and glanced down at his watch. "I'm getting ready to head home too," he said. "I've got big plans tonight—big plans. There's a hotel just down the street from my apartment that has this great seafood buffet every Saturday night—the Hotel Buena Vista. Real fancy place, you know. I'm heading over there in just a bit for the early bird special. I wear my uniform when I go—they always treat me extra special when I'm in my uniform, like I'm a general or something. My favorite dish is the shrimp scampi. Boy, I'll tell you . . ."

Art glanced over at Camille as Phil continued to drone on about the seafood buffet. He didn't want to be rude and glance down at his phone, but he knew they needed to get moving.

"Anyway," Phil continued, "some people like the scallops the best, but not me. Scallops don't really look like anything, am I right? Just sorta blobs. I'm all shrimp all the time. Not as big a fan of those tiny little salad shrimps, though. I always wondered how they peeled those little fellas. Can't be easy, I'll tell you. You ever think about that? Somebody sitting there trying to peel those little suckers. I wonder if they use tweezers. Makes me laugh every time I think about it. But big shrimp? Boy, do I love those. Big and crunchy. Funny, though, my mom was actually allergic to shrimp. If she even got near one, her ears would swell up like a melon. I always wondered how I didn't inherit that. Now, lobster—that's a whole nother . . ."

Art could feel his pulse starting to race. Time was running out. The woman would be coming through the doors into the lobby at any moment. He needed to find some way to end their conversation with Phil—and quick. He ran through a number of excuses in his mind, none of which seemed quite good enough.

Just say something, he told himself.

"Oh my gosh!" Art exclaimed. "I totally forgot about the . . . uh . . . the cat." He looked at Camille. "Your cat—Ms. Fluffers. Don't you need to get home *right now* to . . . do . . . that . . . something . . . for your cat?"

"Oh, right," Camille said. "We need to get home right now. Ms. Fluffers has been sick all week. We need to give her that medicine for her . . . her . . . frecklenosis."

Frecklenosis?

"My goodness," Phil said, "that sounds serious. I've never heard of frecklenosis before."

"It's pretty serious," she said. "And very rare. It makes her . . . uh . . . well . . . it makes her meow backwards."

Meow backwards? Art thought. *Seriously—she just told Phil that her cat meows backwards?*

Phil's eyes went wide. "That sounds terrible," he said. "You don't need to waste your time hanging out here with me—you need to head home right now and make sure Ms. Fluffers gets her medicine."

Camille nodded. "Thank you," she said. "And I'm so sorry we have to rush off like this."

Phil smiled and waved her off. "Don't worry about me," he said. "Just go take care of Ms. Fluffers."

CHAPTER 17

4:40 p.m.
Saturday, April 16
National Portrait Gallery, Washington, DC

Camille and Art turned and hurried toward the exit. They passed through a pair of large double doors, and onto a wide plaza just outside the entrance to the museum. The day had grown overcast, and dark clouds hovered low in the sky. Art paused and glanced back—there was no sign of Phil.

"Frecklenosis?" he asked. "Seriously? And how exactly does a cat meow backwards?"

Camille's face turned bright red. "I couldn't think of anything else to say," she said. "I panicked and it just came out."

"Well, I think it was brilliant," Art said. In Camille's own unique and wonderful way, it had worked perfectly.

"Really?" Camille asked.

"Really," Art replied. "It got us out of there, didn't it?"

A wide smile appeared on Camille's face. Then the smile evaporated. "What time is it?" she asked.

The question caught Art off-guard. "What?"

"Time," Camille repeated. "How much time do we have before the lady leaves the museum?"

Reality immediately set back in for Art. He checked his phone—they had fewer than twenty seconds before the woman made her way out of the museum. But there was a problem. A wide set of stone steps descended from the plaza to the sidewalk below, and then it was at least seventy-five feet to the opposite side of the street. They would never make it across in time.

Art glanced around the plaza for someplace to hide. "There!" he pointed toward a small alcove to the left of the museum entrance, fewer than thirty feet away. Art and Camille sprinted across the landing and into the deep shadows of the recessed space. A moment later the dark-haired woman stepped from beneath the portico and into the plaza. She walked within just a few feet of where Camille and Art had been standing seconds before. Art found himself holding his breath—a completely unnecessary exercise considering the distance between them and the woman.

The woman reached the edge of the plaza and started descending the steps to the sidewalk below. Once she reached the sidewalk, she turned right and started heading east along G Street.

"Let's go," Art whispered.

CHAPTER 18

4:41 p.m.

Saturday, April 16

Washington, DC

Making their way quickly across the plaza, they paused just short of the steps leading down to the sidewalk. The woman was fewer than fifty feet away, her back turned to them as she walked. Art knew they needed to be patient—if they got too close, they risked being spotted. The woman might not recognize him from their previous encounter with the iced mocha, but he couldn't take that chance.

They waited a few more moments—enough time for the woman to make it halfway to the intersection at the end of the block—and then started to descend the steps. Suddenly, however, the woman came to a complete stop. Art and Camille froze.

"What's she doing?" Camille whispered.

As if to answer Camille's question, the woman did something that Art recognized instantly. It was a series of moves that Art witnessed every day in Washington, DC. He had seen people perform this maneuver at restaurants.

At the movies. At the library. At school. At parks. It was performed everywhere and all the time.

The woman first glanced down at her phone and appeared to be sending a text. But Art was convinced that it was not a text. He had seen this tactic too many times to be fooled—he knew exactly what she was doing. His intuition was immediately confirmed when she looked back up, surveyed the street, and then glanced back down at her phone. She repeated this move several times.

Art felt as if he had just been punched in the stomach. All of his plans for the day were about to be completely destroyed.

Art looked at Camille. "She's calling an Uber."

The ridesharing service was used all over Washington, DC. It was easy and convenient—put your destination into the app, and a few minutes later a car would pick you up. He knew that at any moment a vehicle would arrive to whisk the woman off to some unknown location. Camille nodded. It was clear that she had also recognized what was happening.

Art wanted to kick himself. How could he have been so stupid? Sure, Washington, DC, was a great place to walk around, but it also had every imaginable mode of transportation—ridesharing, taxis, buses, subways, trains, and bicycles. But no, he had foolishly believed that the woman would simply walk wherever she was headed, with no regard to the possibility—perhaps the probability—that she would actually use some form of transportation to actually get where she was going.

Stupid, stupid, stupid.

Moments later a large black car pulled up to the sidewalk. The woman opened the back door and got in. They were about to lose their chance—maybe their only chance—to find out where the mysterious woman was headed and get the proof they needed.

The black car pulled away from the curb and up to the intersection at the end of the block. The left-hand turn signal started flashing on the rear of the car. Only the red light on the traffic signal kept the car from immediately disappearing from view—and the light would change any minute.

"We've lost her," Art said.

"Are you kidding me?" Camille said. "You're giving up that easily?"

Art turned to her. "What are we going to do? Run after her?"

There was no way they would ever be able to keep up with the car on foot.

Camille, however, did not seem the least bit dismayed by the circumstances. She smiled and pointed down the steps at the sidewalk below. Art stared at the collection of small machines clustered at the bottom of the steps.

"You're kidding," he said.

Parked there were several electric scooters. There were

thousands of them scattered on sidewalks across the city. They peppered the fronts of museums, monuments, and office buildings, and they could be found in every park in the city. They were available to be rented by anyone who needed them—all that was required was the right app on your phone. Art had seen people zipping all around the city on them, and not just young people—he had seen doctors in scrubs, men and women in business suits, construction workers, gray-haired old ladies, and even a couple of teachers from his school. Art had never tried riding one of the scooters—they seemed like accidents waiting to happen.

The smile remained firmly on Camille's face. "Well," she said, "do you want to follow her or not?"

CHAPTER 19

4:46 p.m.

Saturday, April 16

Washington, DC

After Camille selected one of the scooters from the group parked in front of the museum, she opened an app on her phone and scanned the QR code located near the front of the scooter. A light on the handlebars switched from red to green. Camille tipped the kickstand up with her foot and balanced herself on the scooter.

"Hop on," she said.

Art stared down the street. The black car was still stopped at the intersection at the end of the block. In another moment or so, the light would change and the car would be gone.

"This is such a bad idea," he said as he stepped onto the deck of the scooter behind Camille. He had a vision of them ending up tumbling across the sidewalk—scraped knees, bruises, and possible concussions all in their future.

Art couldn't see Camille's face, but he knew she was grinning.

"Yep," she said. "This is a *very* bad idea."

* * *

Art grabbed Camille around the shoulders. She gently turned the throttle on the handlebar, and the scooter slowly edged along the sidewalk toward the intersection.

Art was impressed. The ride was remarkably solid and smooth, and Camille clearly seemed to know what she was doing. She kept the scooter perfectly balanced as they made their way steadily along the sidewalk.

Art could see the black car waiting at the intersection.

We might just do this, he thought, *as long as the light doesn't*—

And as soon as the thought crossed his mind, the light changed. There was a slight pause, and then the black car started turning left.

We'll never make it now.

But Camille clearly had other thoughts.

"Hold on!" she shouted.

In an instant the scooter lurched forward, Camille hunched over the handlebars and Art hung on for dear life. The scooter now whizzed down the sidewalk toward the intersection. Their problems, however, were far from over. They were approaching the intersection at Seventh Street, and even though they had managed to make it halfway down the block, Art could see the crosswalk signal already counting down from fifteen. There was no way they were going to be able to cross through the intersection before the light changed.

"We're not going to make it!" Art yelled.

Camille ignored him. Instead, she pressed the scooter forward even faster, twisting the throttle on the handlebar as far as it would turn. She zipped around and past the pedestrians on the sidewalk, narrowly missing a schnauzer on a leash. Art caught brief glimpses of the nasty looks the people on the sidewalk gave them as they passed.

"Sorry," Art mumbled over and over again—although he knew none of them could actually hear him.

The crosswalk signal was now down to five, and the orange numbers were furiously flashing.

There was no stopping Camille. Art briefly considered letting go and jumping to safety, but he knew he couldn't. Camille was doing this for him. He was the one who wanted to follow the lady from the museum—and only he fully understood the consequences if they lost her. Maybe she would show back up at the museum tomorrow, but maybe she had already secured all the information she needed. He couldn't take that chance.

No, Camille was right.

Art tightened his grip on Camille's shoulder. Ahead, the black car had cleared the intersection and was starting to make its way north on Seventh Street. It was now or never.

"Push it," Art said.

They hit the crosswalk at full speed just as the crosswalk signal got to zero. The scooter swooped down the small incline from the sidewalk to the roadway and zipped across the wide intersection. Everything was a blur. The wind rushed through his hair, and his nostrils filled with the smells of the city. He could see the familiar red of the city's taxis flashing by in his peripheral vision. He could hear cars beeping and the grinding of a bus's engine as it edged forward in anticipation of the changing traffic light. He watched as the people waiting on the far side of the intersection moved aside to avoid what must have seemed like an inevitable collision. Art's heart was pounding, and he felt as if he was going to fall off at any moment—but the ride was completely, totally exhilarating.

The scooter hit the ramp on the far side of the roadway and hopped up onto the sidewalk. Camille immediately eased up on the accelerator, stuck one foot on the ground, and leaned hard to the left as she whipped the scooter around. Art could feel the scooter skidding across the concrete sidewalk beneath him, and he prepared for the expected crash. But it never came. A moment later, Camille was once more hunched over the handlebars, and the scooter was heading north along Seventh Street, the black car now fewer than fifty feet away.

Camille slowed the scooter down, and they continued along the sidewalk at a more leisurely and discreet pace. Most importantly, they were now in a position to follow the lady from the museum.

"Good job," Art said.

CHAPTER 20

4:50 p.m.

Saturday, April 16

Washington, DC

They managed to keep pace with the black car as it headed north. The low gray clouds had given way to a soft drizzle, and the temperature seemed to have dropped almost ten degrees. Camille's bright red hair—which had been neatly brushed and pulled back with a scrunchie at the start of the day—was now whipping around in all directions as she guided the scooter along the sidewalk.

The traffic lights finally worked in the kids' favor, slowing the black car down just enough for them to stay at a reasonably close distance. Art knew that Camille would follow the car as far as she possibly could (or as far as the scooter's battery would allow), but he also knew that there were limits as to how far they could or should go—they needed to be able to get back home on time to avoid suspicion.

On top of everything else, they still had no clue as to where the woman was headed. Camille's question earlier that morning—about what they would do when the woman finally reached her destination—had haunted him for most of the day. It wasn't as if they were going to follow her into an office with a big sign that read ART THIEVES, INCORPORATED. And there was always the possibility that wherever they ended up would only be a dead-end, or maybe even prove that the lady was not planning the largest art heist in history. Like it or not, he could feel the doubts slowly creeping into his mind. Art took a deep breath and told himself to focus on the task at hand. He could deal with the doubts later.

They followed behind the car for a couple of blocks. Art continued to be impressed by how smoothly Camille handled the electric scooter. And although there had been a few nasty looks from pedestrians along the way, Camille had managed not only to keep up with the black car but to avoid splatting them all over the concrete sidewalk—something that Art greatly appreciated. But the farther they rode, the colder and wetter they became. Camille was taking the brunt of it, and her red hair—damp and frizzled—had appeared to double in size.

As they approached the next intersection, the light turned red and the car came to a stop. Camille slowed down and eased the scooter behind a lamppost. Almost immediately, the turn signal on the passenger's side of the car started blinking.

"They're turning right," Art said, stating the obvious.

Camille—to her credit—refrained from tossing back a sarcastic comment.

The light changed, but Camille remained behind the lamppost and waited until the car had turned the corner before accelerating the scooter down the block. They took a right-hand turn at the intersection and—once more—the rear of the black car was in their sights.

Art scanned the road ahead for any clue as to where the car might be heading. The road was lined with restaurants, coffee shops, office buildings, and hotels—any one of which could be the woman's destination. In truth, Art was starting to feel as if the whole escapade was a bit preposterous. He knew that it had not been particularly well planned, something that fell squarely on his shoulders. He had not anticipated that the woman might be picked up by a car. Moreover, they had spent the past ten minutes following a complete stranger through Washington, DC, in the rain—an act that was quickly starting to feel more like stalking than solving a mystery. Camille had been right—it was sort of creepy.

He suspected that Camille was simply being a good friend—that she didn't fully believe that there was some grand plot to steal paintings from the Millennium Exhibit. He knew it sounded crazy—the story about a mysterious woman and forty-two steps.

But the problem was that he couldn't stop thinking about everything that had occurred over the past week. It had become an earworm of sorts—the song he couldn't get out of his head. He went to bed thinking about it, and he woke up each morning thinking about it. It dominated his thoughts. It demanded his attention. It interfered with his schoolwork. He didn't want to eat. He didn't want to read. And Art knew that until he discovered the truth, that persistent song would continue to play over and over in his head. And so despite the doubts and despite the misgivings, he needed to follow this path wherever it led.

CHAPTER 21

5:02 p.m.
Saturday, April 16
Washington, DC

In Camille's opinion, this endeavor had officially become a wild goose chase. She was cold, wet, and miserable. They had pursued the car for many blocks and yet they were no closer to uncovering where the mysterious woman was headed or who she was—and there was no end in sight to this pursuit. Camille felt that she had been more than patient and that she had done everything a friend could reasonably be expected to do under the circumstances. Chasing the car on the scooter had been exciting for the first few blocks. But she was tired, her shoulders ached, and her hands were numb from gripping the handlebars. With every block, they found themselves farther and farther away from home and more and more likely to get in trouble for venturing so far afield. She could also feel the scooter starting to slow down—the small battery that powered it was close to reaching its limit.

She knew how much all of this meant to Art, but it was time to quit chasing this goose. Whatever the woman may have been up to, Camille was pretty sure that there was no grand conspiracy or plot to steal a billion dollars' worth of paintings from the National Portrait Gallery. The next time they stopped, she would call a halt to the pursuit.

It was time to go home.

But Camille never got the chance to say what she needed to say to Art.

"They're pulling over!" he suddenly exclaimed.

He pointed over her shoulder toward the black car. The light on the rear of the car had started blinking once again, and the car was easing over to the curb. Had the woman reached her destination? Camille brought the scooter to an immediate halt and parked it behind a bus stop in the middle of the block. They watched as the car came to a stop at the curb. Moments later the woman exited the vehicle. She waited until the black car left and then crossed the street.

Camille glanced over at Art. His wet hair was matted against his forehead. He looked as cold and miserable as she felt.

"So?" she asked.

"So we follow," Art replied.

CHAPTER 22

5:05 p.m.

Saturday, April 16

Washington, DC

Art checked the time on his phone—it was now 5:05 p.m. He knew that if the question as to the woman's destination was not answered soon, they would have to turn back toward home. They were expected home by 6:00—any later and their parents would become worried, or suspicious.

"Twenty minutes," Art said to Camille. "We'll give it twenty more minutes and then head home."

Despite the cold and wet conditions, the sidewalk was bustling with people, which provided all the cover Camille and Art needed to follow the woman undetected. They made their way quickly through the crowd, crossed the street, and within moments found themselves trailing close behind her.

It was not exactly the setting that Art had expected. He had envisioned the woman heading to a meeting with some shady-looking character at a clandestine location such as the darkened corner of some fancy hotel lobby or perhaps a bench in one of the city's many parks. There were all sorts of intriguing places in Washington, DC, where the woman could have gone—settings that would have been perfect for a plot to steal a billion dollars' worth of art. Perhaps the steps of the Jefferson Memorial at dusk. Or lost in the mist among the massive plants at the United States Botanic Garden. There was the fountain in front of the Library of Congress. Even a subway platform would have had a certain gritty flair. But the street on which their pursuit was currently taking place lacked any hint of intrigue. They passed a Chinese restaurant, a pizza parlor, a dry cleaner, a small grocery store, and a narrow storefront with a neon sign that advertised the services of Madame English and her psychic readings. There was a row of newspaper racks, a fire hydrant, and a trash can. This was, Art thought, hardly the setting for a grand conspiracy.

Lost in his thoughts, Art did not notice that the woman had now stopped walking. Camille—who had noticed—grabbed Art by the arm and pulled him behind a car parked along the curb. She pointed at the woman, who stood in front of a large building in the middle of the block. It was clearly one of the older buildings in the neighborhood—red brick stained with soot, tall windows with paint flaking from the molding, and a green-tiled mansard roof edged with moss and mildew. A wide stone staircase curved up from the sidewalk to a dark green door flanked on either side by tall, narrow windows. Ornate cast-iron molding framed the entire entrance, and an engraved stone panel set into the brick above the door identified the structure as the J. C. Parker Office Building. A small crack ran the length of the stone panel, neatly bisecting the engraved words. It appeared to Art that the J. C. Parker Office Building may have seen better days.

They watched as the woman went up the steps, unlocked the front door, and stepped inside. Art checked the time on his phone. He still had sixteen minutes to go on his promise. They needed to do something, and the next step was fairly clear.

"We need to get into that building," Art said.

Camille nodded. "I was afraid you were going to say that."

CHAPTER 23

5:09 p.m.

Saturday, April 16

Washington, DC

The rain had finally stopped, but the dark gray clouds and the cold remained. It felt far later in the day than it really was.

"So what's the plan?" Camille asked.

"I need you to go peek through one of the windows next to the front door," Art replied. "See if you can tell what she's doing."

"Me? Why me?"

"Because she's seen me before," Art reminded her. "Maybe she'd remember me. Maybe not. But if she sees you, then no big deal. She'll just think you're some nosy neighborhood kid."

Camille nodded. At this stage, arguing with Art was not worth the effort. Besides, the woman—who was dressed in a business suit—had just entered an office building. It didn't take a genius at this stage to realize what that probably meant: the woman was just like the tens of thousands of other businesspeople who made their way around Washington, DC, every single day—except that she apparently enjoyed a walk through the National Portrait Gallery. Camille held up her phone as she climbed the stairs toward the entrance to the building. The time displayed on the phone was 5:10 p.m.

"Fifteen minutes and we head home," she said.

CHAPTER 24

5:10 p.m.
Saturday, April 16
Washington, DC

Camille made her way up the stairs and eased over to one of the narrow windows next to the front door of the office building. She felt utterly ridiculous spying on the woman, but she also knew it was the only way to really find out if there was some sort of conspiracy to rob the National Portrait Gallery. She took a deep breath and then peeked through the window. Camille immediately spotted the woman. She was standing in front of an elevator at the far end of the lobby, her back to Camille. A moment later the elevator doors opened, and the woman stepped inside. Camille quickly ducked to the side to avoid being seen. When she peeked back through the window, the elevator door had closed. Camille watched as the small digital display above the elevator switched from one to two, two to three, and then three to four, where it stopped.

Camille quickly turned and waved for Art to join her at the front door. Art raced up the stairs and peeked through the side window. Camille pointed to the elevator at the far side of the lobby.

"She went to the fourth floor."

Attached to the exterior wall and next to the front door was a building directory. Adjacent to each name on the directory was a small button—Camille recognized the buttons as part of an intercom system. People visiting the building would use the buttons to contact people in the building, who—in turn—could buzz those visitors inside by remotely unlocking the front door.

The building appeared to have only a handful of tenants—an accounting firm, two law firms, a real estate broker, and a company named Excalibur International Sales and Service, all of which were located on the first three floors. According to the directory, the fourth floor was currently vacant.

Dang, Camille thought.

It would have been so easy if the woman had simply gone to one of the first three floors—the law firm on the second floor, for example. That would have provided at least some explanation as to who the woman was. And truth be told, there was probably a completely reasonable explanation as to why the woman went to the fourth floor. But Camille could already see the thoughts percolating in

Art's conspiracy-riddled brain. She already knew what was coming next.

"We're going to the fourth floor," she said.

Art nodded. "We're going to the fourth floor."

Art reached over and tried the front door.

It was locked, which was not surprising—they had watched the lady use a key to open the door.

"So what now?" Camille asked. "How are you planning to get inside?"

"I need a minute to think," Art said.

Art knew this was not going to be easy, but they had to find some way into the building—and fast. He stepped back from the front door and considered his options.

"Maybe there's a fire escape on the back side of the building," Art said. "We could climb up to the third floor and then go through a window. It would be a little dangerous, but we could do it."

"Couldn't we just—" Camille started to say before she was interrupted.

"Or maybe," Art continued, "we could get into the building next door, go up to the roof, and jump across to the roof of this building. We could then work our way down to the fourth floor."

"Listen, couldn't we just—" Camille said before once again Art interrupted.

"Or maybe there's an old coal chute leading to the basement," Art speculated. "Lots of these old buildings have coal chutes. We just need to find it. We could climb through that into the basement and get into the building."

Camille sighed, walked over to the directory, and pushed the button for Excalibur International Sales and Service. A voice came over the intercom.

"What do you want?" a gravelly woman's voice said.

"I'm meeting someone on the fourth floor," Camille said. "They're not answering—can you buzz me in, please?"

There was a slight pause.

"Sure," the gravelly voice finally replied. "What do I care? Just leave me alone."

"Will do," Camille replied.

A moment later a buzzer sounded and the door clicked.

Art—who had finally stopped talking—stared in disbelief as Camille held the front door open.

CHAPTER 25

5:12 p.m.

Saturday, April 16

J. C. Parker Office Building, Washington, DC

The lobby of the J. C. Parker Office Building—if it could be called a lobby—was little more than a long narrow corridor with a low drop-down ceiling. The floor was linoleum tile—a dingy pale green. The walls were dark wood paneling—the fake kind with the seams that never matched quite right. The air conditioning system hissed and huffed, and the lobby smelled strongly of disinfectant and dust. Art and Camille made their way across the lobby to the single elevator on the far side.

"We can't take a chance with the elevator," Art said. "She might hear us."

He glanced around and then pointed at a door to the left of the elevator. "We'll take the stairs."

Camille checked her phone again. "We have twelve minutes."

Art nodded. "Twelve minutes."

* * *

The stairwell was exceptionally narrow, dimly lit, and poorly ventilated. Made of wood, the stairs creaked and groaned with every step. The sound echoed up and down the stairwell.

Great, Art thought.

It was as if the building were trying to alert the woman to their presence.

They passed the door leading into the second floor. Art peeked through the window on the landing—but it was more of the same green linoleum, low ceilings, and dark wood paneling as the lobby. Art wondered whether that combination had ever looked good. They continued up toward the third floor. It seemed to be at least twenty degrees hotter in the stairwell than in the lobby, and Art found himself wiping sweat from his forehead. He glanced back at Camille.

"Eleven and a half minutes," she whispered.

They paused momentarily on the landing of the third floor.

"So what's the plan when we get up there?" Camille asked.

Art shook his head. "I haven't got that figured out yet," he said.

"Well, you better figure something out soon," she said. "Eleven minutes."

* * *

He could feel his heart thumping in his chest. Art took a deep breath and tried to calm himself. This was not where he had expected to find himself at the end of this day—standing in a dusty, dark, hot stairwell in a rundown office building far away from home.

"Let's do this," he whispered.

Art put his left foot on the first step and tried to place as much of his weight as possible on the thick wooden handrail that ran along the interior of the stairs. This lessened the sound a bit but not quite as much as he had hoped. He stopped every couple of steps, paused, and listened for any sounds from above—for any indication that someone may have heard them. But there was nothing.

Art turned around to look at Camille. He put his index finger to his lips as a signal to Camille to be silent. She pointed at her phone and mouthed the words *Ten and a half minutes.*

He couldn't blame Camille for being anxious. It was late in the day, and she was wet and exhausted. He felt the same way—the adrenaline that was currently running through his veins was the only thing that kept him from just giving up and going home. And besides, he wouldn't have made it this far without her—he owed it to her to get her home on time. He had made a promise, and he intended to keep it. All he wanted was a peek at what was on the fourth floor. Just a peek, and then they would leave.

Moments later they reached the landing in the stairwell on the fourth floor. Sweat was now pouring down Art's face. He took a moment to collect himself and then glanced through the small window on the door leading out of the stairway.

In contrast to the rest of the building, the fourth floor—one big space, almost like a penthouse suite instead of a hallway with different offices—appeared to have been completely renovated. The fake wood paneling, dingy linoleum, and drop-down ceiling had all been removed. The dark claustrophobic feel of the lobby was gone. The floors were now polished hardwood, and shiny metal lights made the vast space glow. It was all quite spectacular. But there was a problem—a big problem. Art had expected to see diagrams, tools, maps—everything that someone would need to plan the world's greatest art heist. But the room was completely empty with the exception of the woman in the blue suit. She stood in the middle of the vast empty space with a large pair of dark goggles on her head. Every so often she would gesture with her arms—as if she were conducting an unseen orchestra in slow motion.

Art stepped back from the window and took a seat next to Camille on the stairs.

"You are not going to believe this," he whispered.

CHAPTER 26

5:16 p.m.

Saturday, April 16

J. C. Parker Office Building, Washington, DC

Art was right.

It was hard to believe what she was seeing.

After peeking through the window, Camille had immediately identified the strange set of goggles that the woman was wearing as a virtual reality headset. There were all sorts of video games that used similar types of goggles. Camille had also spotted a laptop on a small table on the far side of the room—something that Art had completely missed. None of that explained what the woman was actually doing, but it seemed unlikely that she had come all this way just to play some sort of video game.

Camille still was not convinced that the woman was planning an art theft; however, it was equally clear that she wasn't just some random businessperson, lawyer, or tourist.

Something strange was definitely going on.

Camille checked the time on her phone. Art had promised that they would head home in nine minutes. They had to travel all the way across the city to get home by six o'clock and avoid getting into trouble. But the only way to find out what the woman was doing was to get her out of the room and get Art into it.

"Two minutes," Camille said. "If I can get you two minutes alone in the room, will that be enough?"

"But how?" Art asked.

"You'll see," Camille replied. "But two minutes is the best I can promise—maybe not even that long."

Art nodded. If he could get even close to two minutes alone in the room, he would take it.

Camille started to head down the stairs.

"How will I know what to do?" Art asked.

"Trust me," Camille said, "you'll know."

Camille reached the lobby and headed directly for the elevator. She pressed the button and started counting as the elevator started its slow descent to the lobby from the fourth floor.

Five seconds.

Ten seconds.

Fifteen seconds.

Twenty seconds.

Twenty-five seconds.

Ding. The elevator had reached the lobby.

Twenty-nine seconds.

Camille then turned and headed across the lobby, through the front door, and directly out to the sidewalk below.

She immediately started looking on the ground for what she needed.

Old newspaper? Nope.

Crushed soda can? Nope.

Old pizza box? Nope.

Half-eaten burrito? Gross.

A discarded plastic fork?

Camille paused.

A plastic fork could work.

She picked up the fork and carefully bent one of the tines—the pointy parts of the fork—until it broke off in her hand.

Camille held up the small, spiky piece of white plastic.

Perfect.

She made her way back up the steps to the front door. Camille glanced into the lobby. It was empty. She glanced up and down the street. No one seemed to be paying any attention to her. Camille pressed the intercom button for the fourth floor, held it in place, and then wedged the broken fork tine between the button and its casing. The intercom button remained firmly in place.

As nonchalantly as possible, Camille went back down

the stairs and headed across the street toward a bus stop on the far side of the road.

Two minutes, she thought. *You have two minutes, Art.*

Maybe.

Art was still trying to imagine how Camille was planning to pull all of this off when he heard the noise—a ringing sound coming from inside the fourth floor. The sound repeated over and over and over. It took a second for Art to identify the source of the noise, but when he did, a broad grin spread across his face.

It was the intercom button, and it was continuing to ring. Art peeked through the stairwell window. The woman was standing in the middle of the room—she had removed the goggles and appeared visibly agitated at the incessant ringing noise. Art wasn't completely sure how Camille had managed to do this, but it was a genius move.

Art watched as the woman marched over to the intercom next to the elevator, pressed the Call button, and said something into the small speaker. Art couldn't hear exactly what she said through the stairwell door, but he suspected it was not the most friendly of greetings. The ringing stopped momentarily while the intercom button was pressed down and then continued unabated as soon as she lifted her finger.

The woman pounded her fist on the wall and yelled a

word that Art did understand—and could not repeat. Art watched from the stairwell as she pressed the intercom button once more and yelled into the speaker. Again, the ringing stopped as long as the button was pressed but resumed as soon as she lifted her finger.

The woman stood in place for a moment and simply stared at the intercom, as if she did not believe what was happening. She then reached over and pressed the button on the elevator.

Yes!

The woman tapped her foot in frustration as she waited for the elevator. Art watched the small screen above the elevator as it transitioned from one to two, from two to three, and finally from three to four—almost thirty seconds in total. He did the quick math. Two minutes would be pushing it. He needed to be in and out as quickly as possible.

The elevator finally arrived, and the doors creaked open. The woman stepped inside, and a moment later, the elevator started its slow descent to the ground floor.

Art burst through the stairwell door and headed straight for the virtual reality goggles.

CHAPTER 27

5:18 p.m.

Saturday, April 16

J. C. Parker Office Building, Washington, DC

Art lifted the goggles from the table and slipped them on. The padding that lined the edge of the goggles completely cut off any light from the room. He stared out into nothing but darkness. There were obviously no directions as to how to use the goggles. He felt around the outside of the goggles with his hands. His right hand brushed over a small button near his temple. He pushed the button. Light immediately filled the goggles, and it took a moment for his eyes to adjust from the darkness. The image was fuzzy at first —a bit out of focus as his retinas struggled to recover from the sudden onslaught of light. Suddenly everything became clear.

Art gasped.

He was no longer standing on the fourth floor of some rundown office building in Washington, DC—he was standing in the north lobby of the National Portrait Gallery.

* * *

Camille had no idea if her plan had actually worked. She had started counting as soon as she had pushed the button. She guessed that it would take twenty or thirty seconds for the woman to realize that she needed to go downstairs. The trip down the elevator, as Camille knew, would take twenty-nine seconds.

She sat on a bench at the bus stop and waited for the woman to appear at the front door.

Art glanced around. The detail in the virtual reality world was incredible. It was as if he were standing alone in the north lobby of the museum. He could see the gift shop to his right, the information desk directly in front of him, and the elevators on the wall to his left. Directly behind the information desk were the doors leading into the courtyard. There was also something else—something that did not exist in the real world. In the left corner of the lobby—near the ceiling—was a small red circle that simply floated in space. The circle was translucent—like a digital highlighter.

What's that? Art wondered.

He turned and looked around the lobby. There were more floating red circles—four in all—scattered about the room.

Art leaned ever so slightly in the direction of the nearest red circle. This caused him to move forward in the virtual reality lobby. Moments later he found himself standing directly beneath the floating red orb.

Art looked up at the red circle. He realized immediately that he had been right—it was a highlighter of sorts. The red circle marked the position of a device attached to the ceiling—a security camera. He quickly made his way around the room. Each red circle marked a security camera.

Art could feel his heart starting to pound in his chest.

There was something he needed to see, but he was running out of time.

He turned to his right, leaned forward, and headed toward the stairs at the end of the hallway in the Portrait Gallery.

The rain had returned, and the bus stop had quickly grown crowded as people sought shelter. Camille was now squeezed between a man wearing a Nationals jersey and a teenager carrying a skateboard. Camille's internal clock was still running—it had been almost a full minute since she had activated the buzzer. Camille started to wonder whether her plan had worked when the door to the office building suddenly burst open. The woman in the blue suit stepped outside and looked around. She then examined the directory. Camille watched as the woman reached over and removed the fork tine. She then turned and once more looked around, but this time her gaze extended much farther than the immediate vicinity of the building. Camille quickly slid behind the man in the baseball jersey.

Her pulse raced—she found it hard to draw a breath.

A moment later she peeked around the man.

The woman was gone.

Likely headed back to the fourth floor.

Camille pulled out her phone and typed out a quick text message to Art.

"Get out now."

Art had made it to the stairs at the end of the hallway and was climbing quickly to the second floor of the museum. He continued to be amazed at the detail of the virtual reality world. The doors to the second floor opened in front of him as he reached the landing. He stepped into the second floor of the museum. To his right was the west wing. Art turned and leaned in that direction. The farther he leaned forward, the faster he went. He maneuvered his way rapidly through a series of galleries until finally he reached his destination. He stood up straight and came to an immediate stop. Directly in front of him was a large gallery filled with some of the most recognizable paintings in the world. A Rembrandt, a Vermeer, a Degas, a Manet, and a Cassatt.

It was the Millennium Exhibit.

He stepped inside the exhibit gallery and looked around the room. Every camera, every motion detector, and every alarm was highlighted by a floating red circle.

Art understood immediately that this was more than just a set of plans. It was a training program—a platform to practice the theft of a collection of very famous and exceptionally valuable paintings.

Art started to move farther into the room when he felt his phone vibrating in his pocket. He knew what that meant. It was Camille—and it was time to get out.

He reached up to remove the goggles when suddenly something else materialized on the screen in front of him—the word *Message* appeared in bright blue letters. Art knew he was running out of time, but he also knew he would never get this chance again.

It had now been almost twenty seconds since the woman had disappeared back inside. Camille's heart was pounding in her chest. She had no way of knowing what was happening on the fourth floor.

Camille typed out another text message: "GET OUT NOW!"

Art—ignoring the buzzing in his pocket—reached out and touched the word floating in front of him. The screen immediately shifted to what appeared to be a string of text messages. The final message—the one that had just been received—read: "Tomorrow night at 8:00. Final run-through before the gala. Meet at Grognard, DCYC-A17."

His phone vibrated once more in his pocket.

Art reached up and pushed the button on the side of the goggles. The screen immediately went black. He ripped off the goggles and returned them to the table. He glanced over his shoulder at the elevator—the display over the elevator doors flashed from the number three to the number four.

Art sprinted for the door leading into the stairwell.

His hand slipped on the handle as he reached for it, and he almost planted himself face first into the stairwell door.

Bing!

The elevator had reached the fourth floor.

Art reached again, found a firm grip on the handle, opened the door, and slipped behind it, pulling it closed silently behind him.

Camille was about to lose it.

Where are you? she wanted to scream.

It had now been a full minute and there was no sign of Art.

She paced back and forth behind the bus stop. A number of different scenarios—all bad—rushed through her mind.

She pulled out her phone to send another text message and then hesitated. Would that help or hurt him? Again, her mind raced through a million different scenarios—again, all horrible.

She was so distraught that she almost missed the fact that her phone was buzzing in her hand. She looked down. A call from Art.

Camille glanced around, but there was still no sign of him anywhere.

Maybe he had been caught and forced to make the call? Should she answer? What if it was a trap?

Camille hesitated for a moment and then slid her finger across the screen to answer the call.

"Art?" she asked.

There was a slight pause.

Finally, Art's voice responded. "I'm okay. Meet you at the corner near the pizza parlor."

CHAPTER 28

5:24 p.m.

Saturday, April 16

J. C. Parker Office Building, Washington, DC

Catherine Dismuke stood before the window of the fourth floor of the J. C. Parker Office Building and looked out over the street below. It was late in the day, and she was getting hungry. But she had one last item to check off her list before she could head back to her hotel and enjoy a hot dinner.

Dismuke put on the goggles and pushed the power button. The display immediately lit up.

"Call Grognard," she said.

The phone number flashed across the display, and a moment later she could hear the phone ringing through the small speakers built into the headset.

Pizza would be good for dinner, she thought. There was a local pizzeria near her hotel in Georgetown. She could order ahead and carry a pizza back to her room. It had been a long time since she had eaten a pizza by herself, but she had certainly earned the extra calories—it had been a long four weeks in Washington, DC.

There was a click on the line.

"Good evening," a voice said.

"Good evening," Dismuke replied.

"All is ready, I presume?" the voice asked.

"As I promised," Dismuke said. "I saw your message. I'll have the final plans ready for you tomorrow night. You'll be impressed. The security is certainly sophisticated, but I've seen better. There are still plenty of ways to get around it all."

"You've done an excellent job," the voice responded.

There was a slight pause. "And the other matter?" the voice finally asked.

Dismuke chuckled. "The boy?" she said. "He has no idea what he's gotten himself into. Don't worry, we'll resolve that distraction tomorrow night—I guarantee it."

"Very well," the voice replied. "Tomorrow night it is."

There was another click, and the call came to an end.

Or maybe Mexican, Dismuke thought. A nice burrito might be good tonight.

CHAPTER 29

5:25 p.m.

Saturday, April 16

Washington, DC

They hurried toward the Metro station at Mt. Vernon Square, just a short walk from the office building. Art—speaking as fast as Camille had ever heard him—described the virtual reality museum as they walked. Camille could hardly believe what she was hearing.

It was real.

There really *was* a plot to steal the paintings. There was simply no other explanation for what Art had seen inside the virtual reality world on the fourth floor of the J. C. Parker Office Building.

"So what's next?" Camille asked.

"Right before I took off the goggles," Art said, "a message popped up."

"A message?"

"Yeah," Art replied, "and it was weird. There's a meeting tomorrow night. It said they are going to go over the final plans for the theft."

"Wow," Camille replied. "But where?"

"That's the strange part," Art said. "It's going to happen at someplace called the Grognard DCYC-A17—whatever that means. It could be some sort of secret code, but I'm guessing it's an address or maybe a restaurant. I'm not really sure. I'll have to do some research when I get home."

"Grognard DCYC-A17?" Camille asked. She had always been impressed by Art's gift for memorizing details. He could tell you exactly when an artist was born or what year a painting had been completed.

"Yeah," he replied. "Weird, huh? Sounds like a droid from Star Wars."

Actually, Camille thought, *it isn't weird at all.*

"It isn't a restaurant," Camille said, "but it is sort of an address."

"What do you mean, 'sort of an address'?" Art asked. "How can it be sort of an address?"

Camille smiled. She loved it when she knew something that Art didn't.

"The *Grognard* is a boat," she said.

Art came to an immediate stop.

"Wait," he said. "A boat? How could you possibly know that?"

"Don't you know what DCYC stands for?" she asked. "My next-door neighbor has a DCYC bumper sticker—I can't believe you've never seen it. And he has this DCYC T-shirt that he wears all the time when he's running. He actually took me and my mom there once."

Art stood in the middle of the sidewalk and stared at Camille. He seemed genuinely confused, which genuinely amused her.

"It stands for DC Yacht Club," she explained. "It's that fancy boat club down at the Wharf."

Art's eyes went wide. Camille could almost see the light bulb going on above his head.

"Of course," he said. "We walk past that place every time my dad and I go down to the Wharf—it's that big glass building right on the water."

Camille nodded and smiled. "Exactly."

"And A17," Art said. "That's the . . ."

"That's the part of the dock where the boat is . . . well . . . I guess you would say parked," said Camille. "There are, like, three or four docks at the yacht club—A through D, I think. Each boat has its own space on a dock."

"Wow," Art said. "So the *Grognard* is a boat."

"Yep," Camille said triumphantly. "And a boat with the stupidest name I have ever heard. I mean seriously, what the heck is a grognard?"

CHAPTER 30

5:31 p.m.

Saturday, April 16

Washington, DC

They took their seats on the Metro—in the back corner, away from the other five passengers in the car. Camille and Art would be home in twenty minutes. It had been a long day, and Camille was exhausted, wet, and cold. She was looking forward to a hot bath, supper, and a soft bed. She simply wanted to close her eyes and rest, but the day's events kept playing through her mind.

"It all fits," Art said. "All of it."

"What do you mean?" Camille asked.

"Think about the Gardner Museum theft," Art said. "It's like I told you: The thieves needed to know the Gardner Museum backwards and forward—if they hadn't known exactly where they were going when they got inside the museum, they couldn't have pulled it off. And they needed to know all about the security at the Gardner Museum—how many guards would be there, where the security tapes were kept, and where the silent alarm was located."

"And she knows all of that about the National Portrait Gallery," Camille said.

Art nodded. "But the Gardner Museum thieves also needed something else." He paused.

"They needed something to distract the police," Art continued. "The timing had to be perfect—absolutely perfect. The thieves waited until late at night on St. Patrick's Day for a reason—no one would be worried about what was happening at a museum in a quiet section of town. The police had other things to worry about that night."

Art paused again. "Now our thieves have all three. The timing is absolutely perfect."

"Right," Camille said. "They know the museum and all the security and stuff—you saw that in the goggles. And who knows how long the woman had been hanging out at the museum before you ran into her. She probably knows that place better than most of the people who work there. But what do you mean that the timing will be perfect?"

Art sighed. "I didn't tell you before," he said, "but I'm pretty sure I know when they are planning to steal the paintings."

Camille was stunned. That was a pretty big thing to leave out.

"How could you know that?" she asked. "Did you see something in the goggles? Was it another message?"

Art shook his head. "No, but there's only one point when the timing will be just right—the night of the gala."

The night of the gala?

"You have to be kidding," Camille said. "The police will be everywhere at the museum that night. The thieves couldn't pick a worse time to try to steal the paintings."

Art nodded. "You're absolutely right. The police will be all over the museum that night, but they won't be there to protect the art."

Art is right.

"They'll be there to protect the queen," Camille said.

"Exactly," Art replied. "The most important thing the police will be doing that night is protecting the Queen of England. Everything else will be secondary. You heard my dad—the museum has all of that high-tech security in place, and they completely trust it. They have no idea that someone knows all about it. So while everybody is focused on the queen . . ."

"The thieves steal a billion dollars' worth of art," Camille said. "Including a Rembrandt, a Vermeer, a Manet, and a Degas—just like the Gardner Museum."

CHAPTER 31

5:33 p.m.
Saturday, April 16
Washington, DC

It was now clear to Camille that there was something else Art had not told her. Something that was even more unimaginable than a plot to steal a billion dollars' worth of art.

"You think this has something to do with what happened at the Gardner Museum, don't you? More than just another big art heist?" she asked.

"I do," Art replied. "I think it may be the same people. I didn't want to say anything because . . ."

"Because it sounds so crazy," Camille said.

Art nodded.

Camille considered what Art had just suggested. The possibility that the same people who had stolen all of the artwork from the Gardner Museum might be the same people who were planning to rob the National Portrait Gallery seemed far-fetched. But was it as far-fetched as what Camille and Art had just discovered in an old office building in Washington, DC? It seemed as though anything was possible at this stage.

"Why do you think it's the same people?" Camille asked.

"The Gardner Museum theft happened way before I was born," Art said, "but I've read all about it. I've been to the Gardner Museum. I've seen the empty frames. I've walked the exact same hallways and stairs the thieves walked. Everything about this reminds me of the Gardner Museum theft. The artwork in the Millennium Exhibit: a Rembrandt, a Vermeer, a Degas, a Manet. Those are the exact same artists that the thieves went after at the Gardner Museum. And the timing of it all—almost exactly thirty years after the Gardner Museum theft and on the night of the queen's visit. The precision and planning that it would require to pull all of this off would be incredible—just like the Gardner Museum."

Art paused. "And there's something else."

"What?" Camille asked.

"It didn't take just planning to rob the Gardner Museum," he said. "It took . . . arrogance. It was arrogant to believe that something that impossible could actually happen. How many people on this planet would have the ability, the resources, and the arrogance to actually rob the Gardner Museum? How many people would have the arrogance to spend eighty-one minutes in the Gardner Museum with absolutely no fear of getting caught?"

"Not many," Camille agreed.

"Exactly," Art replied. "That's another reason why I

think the people who planned the Gardner Museum heist are the same ones planning this one. They did it once, and they have the arrogance to do it again."

If Art was right, then what they had stumbled upon was far more dangerous than Camille had ever considered. The people who committed the Gardner Museum theft had managed to evade capture for thirty years, and none of the paintings from the Gardner Museum had ever been recovered. These were smart people. They were prepared. They were ready to overcome any obstacle. And they weren't going to let a couple of kids get in their way.

"So why not just tell your dad?" Camille asked. "Just go ahead and tell him what you saw this afternoon. Tell him about the woman. Tell him about the mocha. Tell him about the forty-two steps. Tell him about the goggles. Tell him about the *Grognard*. Tell him that you think these are the same people who robbed the Gardner Museum. Just tell him—he'll believe you."

Art shuffled in his seat. "That's what I'm afraid of," he replied. "I'm afraid he will believe me. I'm afraid he'll go to the people in charge at the museum and tell them what I've seen."

"And what's wrong with that?" Camille asked. "Isn't that what you want?"

"Just think about that," Art said. "How would my dad explain the forty-two steps? Or how his son spent all day following some mysterious woman around the city? Or about a set of goggles that re-create a super accurate virtual reality version of the museum? We don't have any pictures. We don't have the goggles. We don't have any videos. We have nothing but what I saw. And then—to top it all off—he tells them that it's all related to the Gardner Museum heist, the most famous art theft in history. How do you think the people at the museum will react to all of that?"

Camille knew exactly how a bunch of grownups would react when they heard all of that.

"They would think it's a big joke," she said.

Art nodded. "Yep. A big joke. I would be a joke, and my dad would be a joke for believing me. I can't put him in that position, especially since he just started this job. That's why I've got to get to that boat tomorrow night. I need proof—and that's where it will be. Everyone will be there—the woman, her accomplices, and all the plans for robbing the museum. All of it in one place."

Art sighed.

"I'm just not sure how I'm going to get there without getting into a whole lot of trouble," he said.

"Actually," Camille replied, "I've been thinking about that while you've been feeling sorry for yourself. I think I can get us to the boat tomorrow night without anyone getting in trouble."

Art sat up in his seat. "You can? But how?"

Camille merely smiled. "You like oysters, right?"

CHAPTER 32

7:37 p.m.

Saturday, April 16

Hamilton residence, Washington, DC

Art's father was an excellent cook. The scent of yellow chicken curry—his father's specialty—drifted from the kitchen into the living room, where Art sat and tried to work on a project that was due at school the following Monday.

Normally, the smell of his father's homemade curry would immediately set his stomach growling. But this evening was different—eating was the last thing on Art's mind.

"Almost ready!" his father yelled from the kitchen. "I hope you're hungry!"

"Can't wait!" Art yelled back, trying his best to sound enthusiastic despite the complete lack of an appetite. It had been an hour and a half since he had gotten home, and he had still not heard from Camille. She had assured him that she could get them to the boat the following evening but had provided no details as to how she would manage to pull it off. Art trusted Camille, and he knew that she was extremely resourceful. She was the one who had thought of following the woman on the scooter. She was the one who had managed to get him some time alone on the fourth floor of the office building. He knew what Camille was capable of, but that didn't make the waiting any better.

Art leaned back on the couch and tried to focus on the school project in front of him.

It was useless.

His brain refused to cooperate.

Every time he tried to focus on the project, his brain would immediately divert his thoughts to the Millennium Exhibit. And now that it was no longer speculation on his part—now that there was unquestionably a plot to steal paintings from the National Portrait Gallery—his brain was in some sort of supercharged overdrive.

What he had seen in the virtual reality goggles played over and over again in his mind. He had walked step by step through the woman's virtual reality world. She knew all of the museum's defenses—every security camera, every motion detector. And he knew that others were involved—the message that the woman had received proved that. The conspiracy was real and perhaps far bigger than he had dared to consider.

And yet, he still had nothing.

It was still his word against . . . whose? A mysterious woman from the museum whom he and Camille had followed to some creepy old building? And even though he knew exactly where the people conspiring to steal the paintings would be, he still didn't have any plan for actually getting there and finding the proof he needed. He checked his phone for any messages from Camille, on the off chance that he might have missed a call or text from her.

Nothing.

"Here it comes!" Arthur Hamilton Sr. exclaimed as he entered the living room. He was carrying a large bowl full of yellow chicken curry and rice, which he plopped down on the coffee table in front of Art.

"Thanks, Dad," Art replied.

Art's father paused and stared down at his son.

"Is something wrong? You seem distracted."

His father knew him too well. Art wouldn't be able to keep this from him for much longer. He desperately wanted to tell his father everything. He could practically feel the words bursting to get out. But he also knew what might happen if he did. He had to keep the words inside a bit longer.

"Just school," Art said. "I have a big project I'm working on—but it should be finished by tomorrow night. I just need to focus."

"Well, take your time and get it done right," his father said, "but try to finish it up by six o'clock tomorrow. We've got plans for tomorrow evening."

"Plans?"

Great.

Another complication.

"Yep," Arthur Sr. replied. "Camille's mom called and

asked us to join them for dinner tomorrow night—they want to thank us for getting them invited to the gala. I told her they didn't have to do that, but she insisted."

Dinner? Art perked up immediately. Was this part of Camille's plan?

"Where are we going?"

"Down to the Wharf," his father replied. "Mary got us reservations for six thirty at Hank's Oyster Bar."

Art did his best to keep from grinning. Camille had done exactly what she had said she would do—they would be down at the Wharf when the meeting was going to take place. Exactly what they would do when they got down there remained unclear, but one step at a time. Besides, when did a lack of a plan ever stop them?

All of a sudden his father's yellow chicken curry smelled great.

CHAPTER 33

7:40 p.m.

Sunday, April 17

Hank's Oyster Bar, Washington, DC

Situated along the Washington Channel—a narrow waterway just north of the confluence of the Potomac River and the Anacostia River—the Wharf was a collection of trendy restaurants, boutique hotels, and retail shops that had become a popular Washington, DC, hot spot. Families gathered along the pier each evening to watch the sun set, and there always seemed to be something happening at the concert venues located along the water. There was even a small kiosk that sold the ingredients for s'mores—and a handy fire pit over which the marshmallow and chocolate snack could be cooked. And on top of all of that, the Wharf was home to Hank's Oyster Bar—the best place to get oysters in the entire city.

Art, Camille, Arthur Hamilton Sr., and Mary Sullivan stared out over a pile of empty plates spread across their table on the patio overlooking the waterway. They lingered at the table enjoying the cool night air. For a very brief period of time, Art had managed to forget about the conspiracy to rob the museum and enjoyed the meal and the company. He had sometimes wondered whether his father had really wanted to settle down in Washington, DC, or if it was something he had done out of a sense of obligation to Art. But sitting there at the table and watching his father, Art could tell that his father was enjoying life in DC as much as Art was—and Art didn't want that to change. He glanced down at his phone and then over at Camille. In twenty minutes the meeting would be taking place on the boat. It was time to get going.

"Do you mind if Camille and I walk around a bit?" Art asked. "Maybe get an ice cream or something?"

Arthur Hamilton Sr.—who looked more than content to just sit there and enjoy the spring air—looked over at Mary Sullivan. "Any objection?"

Mary Sullivan shook her head. "No objection, but we need to head home by eight thirty, okay? The two of you have school tomorrow."

"Got it," Camille replied. "Meet you at the pier at eight thirty?"

"Eight thirty it is," Mary Sullivan said.

There was a concert that evening at the Anthem, a large music venue on the Wharf, and the pedestrian walkway was crowded with scores of twenty-somethings. Camille and Art made their way quickly along the cobblestone path in the direction of the glass and steel building sitting on the edge of the water. Art could see the words DC YACHT CLUB emblazoned on the side of the building. Jutting out from the back of the yacht club and into the channel were four long docks. A variety of boats were moored in slips along the docks—houseboats, sailboats, cabin cruisers, boats that appeared to be designed primarily for fishing, and a handful of large boats that could truly be described only as yachts. But there was one boat that stuck out from all the rest—a massive white boat moored at the very end of the westernmost dock. And although Art could not see the name of the boat due to the distance and the dimming light, he knew exactly what it was—the *Grognard*.

Camille had done a great job getting them to the Wharf and this close to the boat, but two huge hurdles remained. First, the DC Yacht Club was a private club, which meant that access to the docks was limited to members only. And second, even assuming they could make it past the club's security and onto the docks, they still had to find some way onto the boat itself. Camille, however, had already assured him that she had a plan, but—yet again—she had offered no additional explanation as to how she intended to get them onto the docks and then onto the boat.

Moments later they found themselves standing on the far side of the pedestrian walkway and directly opposite the front entrance of the yacht club. The only way they could get to the docks was directly through the front entrance

—unless Camille was planning to jump into the water and swim. Art checked the time on his phone—the meeting was scheduled to take place in ten minutes. They needed to get into the yacht club, past the security desk, and to the boat as soon as possible.

"So what's the plan?" Art asked. "How are we getting through security and to the docks?"

"We're not," Camille replied.

Art's jaw dropped. "What do you mean, 'we're not'? We have to get on those docks."

Camille shook her head. "We don't have to get on the docks. We can get to the boat without going through the yacht club."

She's actually going to swim there, Art thought. This had officially become a disaster. They were about to blow their only chance to get the proof they needed.

"We don't have time for this," Art said. "We have to find some way onto those docks."

Camille calmly took off her backpack and opened it up so that Art could see inside.

"That's how we're getting to the boat," she said. "Without going through the yacht club or getting on the docks."

Art was dumbfounded.

How had he not thought of that?

"Camille," he said. "You're a genius."

CHAPTER 34

7:52 p.m.

Sunday, April 17

The Wharf, Washington, DC

At the far end of the Wharf and directly opposite the dock at which the *Grognard* was moored was the Market Pier. The Market Pier sat adjacent to a massive seafood market located in the shadows of the Francis Case Memorial Bridge. The outdoor seafood market and the pier were the only reminders of the Wharf's former life—a time when the people who roamed the waterfront were deck hands, sailors, and dock workers, not families, tourists, and millennials. The pier lacked the amenities of the rest of the Wharf—it remained a working dock. It was used by fishing boats and crabbers who brought their catches to market. It smelled of baitfish, rotting seaweed, and salt water. There were few lights, and there was no security gate. The Market Pier had none of the piped-in music that floated from hidden speakers along the rest of the Wharf. It was dark, and there were no tourists. It was perfect.

Art and Camille made their way to the far end of the pier and settled on a narrow side dock that directly faced the bright lights and fancy trappings of the DC Yacht Club. They sat at the end of the dock, two small fishing boats on either side of them. The lights on the houseboats and yachts glimmered in the water of the channel. Camille opened her bag and retrieved the small device. She handed it to Art.

It was a small drone equipped with a high-definition video camera.

"You know how to use it?" Art asked.

Camille laughed. She had received the drone as a gift the previous Christmas, and it had already been deployed on several missions. She had used it at home to check on dinner several times—navigating the small device down the stairs, through the living room, and into the kitchen. She had used it during a snow day back in January to see if the road at the end of their block had been cleared. And she used it to make videos of her cat. Ms. Fluffers absolutely hated the drone.

The drone operated through an app on her phone, had ten minutes of flight time on a full charge, and was self-stabilizing. Camille could pilot it through an opening the size of a mailbox without touching the sides. It was remarkably quiet and deceptively fast. The video it produced was amazing. Getting it over to the boat would be a snap.

"Yes," she assured him. "I know how to use it."

* * *

"Five minutes until eight o'clock," Art said.

They had decided to wait until the woman appeared before sending over the drone. With only ten minutes of flight time, they had to be careful in how they used it. The good news was that the drone was dark blue—which would make it almost impossible to see against the dark water or the night sky—and the noise from the Wharf and the channel would easily mask the slight hum of the four fan blades that powered the small device's flight.

The yacht had been moored perpendicular to them, and they had a full view of the left-hand side—the port side—of the boat. (Art had explained that he could always remember that the port side was the left side of a boat because both "left" and "port" had only four letters.) The yacht was beautiful—it had a sleek aerodynamic design, almost like a giant racing boat or spaceship. It was painted white with a giant blue stripe down the side, and the word *Grognard* was written in script on the front edge of the vessel. Art guessed that the yacht was probably around eighty or ninety feet long—easily the biggest boat docked at the Wharf that evening. It had three levels: an upper level with a deck and the captain's bridge, a middle level with windows that ran almost the length of the boat, and a lower level with a couple of small portholes that sat just above the water line. There were several lights on in the middle level and there appeared to be some movement, but the distance was too far to make out any details.

A slight breeze rolled across the water, and the moon—though not completely full—provided more than enough illumination for Camille to safely guide the drone across the water to the yacht when it was time. Art and Camille sat in silence and simply listened to the water lapping against the fishing boats.

They didn't have to wait long.

"She's here!" Camille suddenly exclaimed. She pointed at the dock leading to the *Grognard*. A woman was making her way down the pathway, followed by two men carrying large black cases. And although it was too far to see her face, the way the woman was walking was unmistakable—the same measured, precise walk Art had seen for the past week at the National Portrait Gallery.

His heart jumped in his chest.

All of the pieces were falling into place.

CHAPTER 35

8:00 p.m.

Sunday, April 17

The Wharf, Washington, DC

Camille placed the drone on the edge of the dock. It was about the size of a small paperback book and little more than an inch thick. It had four propellers located at the end of hinged arms that folded over on top of the body for storage. Camille unfolded the propellers and locked the arms in place. She then opened the drone app on her phone.

"Ready?" she asked.

"Ready," Art replied.

Camille pressed the Start button on the app. The drone hummed to life and rose about a foot into the air. Art started the timer on his phone.

"Ten minutes counting down," he said.

The drone hovered over the dock like a retriever waiting for a stick to be thrown. With her right thumb, Camille gently nudged the toggle on the app forward—the drone responded by edging out over the water. The device shimmied for a moment in the breeze and then stabilized itself. Camille smiled and pushed the toggle all the way forward.

In an instant the drone was buzzing across the water toward the yacht.

The drone disappeared into the inky darkness almost immediately.

For a moment Art was concerned that the drone may have taken an immediate nosedive into the water. He leaned over and looked at the screen on Camille's phone. To his relief, he could see the boat rapidly approaching. The video on the screen was remarkable—it was like watching a high-definition movie. If this worked, they would be able to secure all the proof they needed. Art envisioned sending the incriminating video directly to his father. Perhaps the police or the FBI would show up that very evening. And perhaps they would not only prevent the biggest art theft in history but actually solve the Gardner Museum heist.

"Good job," Art said to Camille.

The drone was flying just a few feet above the water—they had decided it would be best to approach from that angle to avoid detection. Camille brought the drone to a hover about thirty feet away from the yacht. Art checked the timer on his phone. It had taken just more than thirty seconds to reach the boat.

"Nine minutes and twenty-five seconds left," he said.

Plenty of time.

They had lost sight of the woman and the two men when they had passed behind the boat on the dock, but there had now been ample time for the three of them to make their way onboard. Art could see the top deck of the boat from where he and Camille were sitting—it appeared to be completely empty.

Good.

That narrowed down their search.

"Let's check the middle level first," Art said.

Camille maneuvered the drone toward the front end of the yacht, stabilized it so that it was even with the windows on the middle level, and then started moving it parallel to the massive ship—far enough away to remain undetected but close enough to see what was going on inside. The wind had started to pick up a bit, and the video feed—although crystal clear—had become a bit shaky. Camille was forced to move far slower than Art would have liked to keep the camera as steady as possible.

Art checked the timer on his phone. "Seven minutes and twenty seconds to go," he said. They had covered almost a quarter of the ship with no sign of the woman or the mysterious owner of the *Grognard*.

A knot was starting to form in Art's stomach—an all-too-common occurrence over the past week. What if they couldn't get the proof they needed? What then? Should he just go ahead and tell his father? Art knew he had no choice

—he would have to tell him what he knew. Art couldn't allow the gala to proceed, knowing what the thieves were planning. But absent any real proof, his father would be in an impossible position.

Art checked the time on his phone. "Six minutes and twelve seconds," he announced. They had now covered half the ship with no sign of anyone.

The wind had continued to pick up, and the video feed had become even shakier.

"We've got a problem," Camille said. She pointed at the monitor on her app. The power bar had suddenly dropped below twenty-five percent—far lower than it should have been. Art recognized the issue almost immediately.

"The drone is eating up power trying to stay stabilized," he said.

The increasing wind was drawing down the small drone's battery far quicker than expected. Art realized that they now had fewer than two minutes to find their targets. He immediately updated his timer to reflect the new countdown.

CHAPTER 36

8:04 p.m.

Sunday, April 17

The Wharf, Washington, DC

Camille stared intensely at the small screen, searching for any sign of movement through the small windows that ran the length of the yacht. They had now made it almost three-quarters down the side of the vessel with no sign of anyone.

She glanced at the small power bar in the top right-hand corner of the screen. It had turned from green to yellow. Once it hit five percent, the drone would automatically return to Camille. The yellow bar meant they had barely more than a minute to locate the woman.

Art glanced down at his phone. One minute and thirty-seven seconds to go. The knot in his stomach had grown tighter and tighter. They were running out of time.

* * *

Camille moved the drone as quickly as she could—the video feed had grown increasingly shaky, but they had little choice. They had covered almost ninety percent of the ship with no sign of—

Whoa!

"Hey, hey, hey!" Camille exclaimed. "I think I've got something!"

Art, who had been looking over her shoulder, had seen it as well. There was movement from within the ship—several dark shapes shifting around. But they were too far away to get a clear shot of what was taking place.

"We need to get closer," Art said.

Camille glanced at the power bar—it had now reached ten percent. The time was now or never. She pushed the toggle forward.

Art watched on the video screen as the drone got closer to the yacht. The image was still far too shaky to make out any details. He checked his timer—they were now down to less than a minute.

Suddenly the drone came to a stop and stabilized against the increasing wind. The image—which had been little more than flashes of light against a dark background—became clear. They were looking directly into the yacht, the drone being little more than a few feet from the window.

Art's heart jumped in his chest. The woman stood in

front of a large television screen, and on a small table in front of the television were the goggles they had seen back at the J. C. Parker Office Building. The two men who had accompanied her stood on the far side of the room. Sitting directly in front of the woman was a man. Art could see him only from behind—a full head of silver hair. But it was the image on the screen that caused Art's pulse to race. It was a picture of a Rembrandt portrait—the same self-portrait that was to be displayed in the Millennium Exhibit in less than a week. It had been painted in 1659. It showed the artist sitting sideways and looking at the viewer over his left shoulder. Rembrandt's gray hair billowed out from beneath a dark beret. The paint was thick, and the tone was dark. It was a portrait of an artist at the height of his career.

The screen flashed to a new image—the Degas portrait, the same as in the exhibit. And then to the Vermeer—the girl with the red hat. And then to the Manet.

It was the Gardner Museum all over again.

Camille gasped.

There it was—all of it.

The screen flashed from an image of the Manet to the floor plan of the museum.

Art had been right.

"Please tell me you've been recording," Art said.

Camille glanced down at the app on her phone. Everything was being recorded.

A broad smile crossed her face.

"I've got it," she said. "All of it."

At that moment, the power bar on the app turned red, and the video on the drone immediately shifted away from the yacht.

The drone was returning home.

They had done it.

CHAPTER 37

8:08 p.m.
Sunday, April 17
The Wharf, Washington, DC

The drone landed with a clunk at Camille's side just as the power bar on the app reached zero.

"Good job," she said, and patted the small mechanical device.

It was now 8:08 p.m. They still had almost twenty minutes before they had to meet her mother and Art's father.

"We need to send the video to my dad," Art said. "We still might be able to catch them while they're all on the boat."

Camille nodded. "Sending you the video now," she replied. She had already opened the photos app on her phone and was preparing to text the video to Art. The video file was large, but Camille knew that Art would want it in full HD. She pushed Send on her text.

"It will be there in a minute or so," she said.

Camille put her phone down and leaned back on the dock. Back in December, when she had helped Art regain his memory and stop an international art forgery ring, there had been little fanfare. The National Gallery of Art had —not surprisingly—preferred to downplay the fact that two kids had saved them from spending one hundred and eighty million dollars on a fake Van Gogh painting. Not that Camille needed recognition—though a little would have been fine.

But now? They were about to prevent the theft of a *billion* dollars' worth of famous paintings and, if Art was correct, solve the biggest art theft in history.

Not bad for a couple of kids.

A little publicity might be in order.

Maybe the front page of the *Washington Post,* or an interview on *Entertainment Tonight.* Either would do.

There was a *ping* as the text arrived on Art's phone. The video and a full explanation of how they had caught the bad guys would soon be on the way to Art's father.

Camille looked over and smiled.

I can't wait to put this on Instagram, she thought.

"You really shouldn't spy on folks," a man's voice said. It had come from behind them.

Camille's heart dropped in her chest.

She turned around to find two large men standing directly behind them.

"We were . . . uh . . . just . . . s-sitting here," Art stuttered.

"You were just spying on my employer," the man said. "And he's not happy about it."

The man bent down and put his hand out. "Cell phones. Now."

Camille glanced over at Art. They were sitting at the edge of a dock, far away from the crowds that made their way up and down the Wharf. They had chosen the spot because it was isolated. It had been perfect for what they needed to do. But now they were isolated from those same crowds. They could have screamed all they wanted, but there was no way they would have been heard. The sounds from the Wharf, the wind, and the sloshing of the waves presented an impenetrable barrier. And there was nowhere to run—the two men stood between them and solid ground. Camille and Art were simply small dark blobs in the silent distance. They were trapped.

"Give him your phone," Art said as he handed his phone to the man. Camille did the same.

The second man gestured toward a boat that had been pulled alongside the dock behind them. Camille wondered how long the dinghy had been there—how long the two men had been watching them.

"Into the boat," the man instructed.

CHAPTER 38

8:19 p.m.

Sunday, April 17

The Wharf, Washington, DC

Art and Camille sat on a long leather couch in the same room on the yacht that they had filmed with the drone. The room was far bigger than Art had expected and appeared to be a library of sorts. The walls of the room were lined with dark mahogany paneling and bookshelves. Each bookshelf had a bronze bar running across the middle to prevent the books from spilling out in turbulent seas. Several paintings and engravings hung on the walls. Art recognized at least one of the paintings as the work of a minor Renaissance painter—not exactly a Botticelli, but impressive nonetheless.

They had been taken aboard the yacht by the two men who had confronted them on the dock and then placed in the room without any additional conversation or further word of explanation. The image of the museum's floor plan remained on the large-screen television at the far end of the room. The two large black cases that the men had carried onboard sat beneath the television. And sitting on the coffee table directly in front of them was the pair of virtual reality goggles that Art and Camille had first seen back at the J. C. Parker Office Building. There did not seem to be any effort to hide what was happening. Art did not consider that a particularly good sign.

Sitting directly in front of them in a large wingback chair was the silver-haired man they had seen on the drone video. Next to him sat the woman that they had followed the previous day. Neither the man nor the woman had said a word since Camille and Art had been brought into the room and placed on the couch. The woman was typing into her phone. A few moments later, she finished typing and nodded at the man.

The man leaned forward in his chair. He was thin and wore a nicely tailored dark blue jacket with a white button-down shirt. He had a deep bronze tan and his hair was neatly combed, with not a single silver strand out of place. The man was not smiling, and he did not seem the least bit amused.

"You should have minded your own business," he said.

He spoke slowly, emphasizing each word.

"This is not a matter for children," he added. "You have no idea what is at stake."

Children? Art thought.

Who was this guy kidding? Art and Camille had been trying to prevent the theft of some of the most important works of art on the planet. A Rembrandt, a Vermeer, a Degas, a Cassatt, a Manet—and so much more. Scared or not, Art wasn't about to back down from this man.

"My dad will be looking for us any minute now," Art said. "You'd better let us go."

And even though he felt as though he might throw up, the strength and determination in his own voice surprised him.

The silver-haired man did not seem disturbed or concerned. He glanced over at the woman.

"The call has been made?" he asked.

The woman nodded. "He'll be here any moment." She spoke with a slight British accent.

"Very well," the silver-haired man replied. He gestured toward Art and Camille. "We'll let him deal with this . . . inconvenience. Our plans will proceed forward as we discussed."

There was a *ping* on the woman's phone—the unmistakable signal of a text message. She glanced down at it. "He's onboard," she said.

The silver-haired man stood up. He went over to one of the windows overlooking the channel and gazed out at the night sky. His back was turned to them. "You should not have interfered in my business," he said, his tone pointed and businesslike. "Appropriate steps will need to be taken."

Camille gasped.

"What . . . s-steps?" she stammered. "What's going to happen to us?"

The man did not respond. He stood and continued to gaze out the window.

"You won't get away with this," Art blurted out. It was a stupid thing to say, and Art knew it—it sounded like something out of *Scooby-Doo.* But false bravado and a healthy dose of adrenaline were the only things that were keeping him going at this point. Otherwise he would have been projectile-vomiting his dinner out of sheer fear.

There was a knock on the door.

"He's here," the woman said.

Art glanced over at Camille. Her eyes were tinged with red, and she looked as if she might burst out crying at any moment. He didn't blame her—he could feel the emotions welling up inside of him as well. He had dragged Camille into this whole situation. He was responsible for what was happening.

"I'm sorry," he said to Camille.

Camille opened her mouth to respond, but there were no words.

The door opened.

Art gasped.

It couldn't be.

Not him.

CHAPTER 39

8:22 p.m.
Sunday, April 17
The Wharf, Washington, DC

"Dad?" Art exclaimed. "What are you doing here?"

Art couldn't believe what he was seeing.

Arthur Hamilton Sr. stood in the doorway of the yacht and stared across the room at his son. What was his father doing on the *Grognard*? The past week flashed through Art's mind—the iced mocha, the forty-two steps, the J. C. Parker Office Building, the virtual reality glasses, the similarities between the paintings in the Millennium Exhibit and the works of art stolen from the Gardner Museum, and what he and Camille had just witnessed taking place on the yacht. Everything led to one inescapable conclusion—that someone on this boat was planning to steal a billion dollars' worth of paintings from the Millennium Exhibit. And yet standing here—directly in front of him—was his father?

Nothing made sense.

Without saying a word, Art's father stepped into the room. He was followed by Mary Sullivan.

It was Camille's turn to gasp.

"Mom?"

Mary Sullivan, unlike Art's father, did not remain silent. "You are in so much trouble."

Art glanced over at Camille. All the blood had drained from her face. It was the first time that Art had ever seen Camille's mother mad. It was pretty frightening.

Art took a deep breath and tried to take in everything that was happening. There had to be some sort of logical explanation. Maybe the woman and the silver-haired man had kidnapped his father and Mary Sullivan. Or maybe they were tricking them into being part of the plot to rob the museum. There was only one thing to do—he had to tell his father what he knew.

Art opened his mouth to explain what had happened, but his father raised his hand to silence him. "Don't make this any worse than it already is."

Worse?

Arthur Hamilton Sr. gestured toward the silver-haired man.

"Arthur," his father said, "I would like to introduce you to Ludwig Hoggard III."

"Uh-oh," Camille immediately said.

Art looked at Camille.

What did she mean by that?

Who was Ludwig Hoggard III?

The silver-haired man looked at Camille. "You recognize my name."

Camille nodded. "From the invitation to the Millennium Exhibit gala," she replied. "I keep it next to my bed—I read it every night."

The invitation to the gala? Art could not recall if he had ever actually seen the invitation.

"That's correct," Arthur's father said. "Mr. Hoggard is the founder of the Hoggard Trust for the Arts—the sponsor of the Millennium Exhibit."

Uh-oh, thought Art.

Art's father gestured to the woman sitting on the couch. "And this is Catherine Dismuke," he said, "one of the foremost security experts on the planet. She was hired by Mr. Hoggard to test the security at the National Portrait Gallery in advance of the Millennium Exhibit. He wanted to make absolutely certain that the security at the museum was being handled properly. Only a handful of people knew what she was doing."

Oh no.

Art's mouth went dry, and his palms started to sweat. This was not going the way he'd thought it would.

Catherine Dismuke leaned forward on the couch. A slight smile creased her face. "I must say," she said, "that I am quite impressed by what the two of you managed to do."

Her soft British accent was not what Camille had expected but seemed completely fitting under the circumstances in which they now found themselves. It was very spylike.

"Bravo for spotting me at the museum," Dismuke said to Art. "No one else seemed to take notice."

Dismuke glanced over at Hoggard. "I've included that in my report, by the way," she said. "I tried to be as obvious as possible—I walked through at the exact same time each day for two weeks and followed the exact same path each day. This young man was apparently the only one who seemed to think that was odd."

Mr. Hoggard simply nodded. He still did not seem amused.

Catherine Dismuke turned to Art and Camille. "And then managing to track me halfway across the city to the office building showed some real determination—and in the rain on a scooter, no less. And the drone? Don't even get me started—that was an absolutely brilliant idea."

"My idea," Camille said with a smile—a smile that immediately vanished thanks to a withering look from her mother.

"All of that is beside the point," Arthur Hamilton Sr. said. "The two of you broke into Ms. Dismuke's office, rummaged through her property, and then used a drone to spy on her and Mr. Hoggard. That is totally unacceptable."

The disappointment was clear in his father's voice, and

that stung. But Art also felt that his father was not being completely fair.

"But I thought she was planning to rob the museum," Art said. "All the clues pointed toward that. What was I supposed to do?"

"You were supposed to tell me," his father replied. "And the fact that you didn't hurts the most."

Art looked down at the floor. There was nothing else he could say. He had never felt so embarrassed and angry in his life. He had agonized over the decision not to say anything to his father. Art had thought he was protecting his father by waiting until he had actual proof that the plot was real. But it turned out that it was all a ruse — nothing more than an effort to test the security at the National Portrait Gallery.

He hadn't saved his father from embarrassment.

He had become the embarrassment.

CHAPTER 40

8:35 p.m.

Sunday, April 17

The Wharf, Washington, DC

Camille and Art sat on the couch while her mother and his father discussed the situation with Mr. Hoggard and Catherine Dismuke in the adjoining room. He had no idea what to expect. All sorts of different scenarios raced through his mind. Everything he had done now seemed so foolish.

He had been so sure of himself—so confident in his own conclusions. Even worse: he had actually believed that all of what was happening was somehow tied to the theft at the Gardner Museum, a crime that had been committed thirty years ago. In retrospect, it all seemed so completely, utterly stupid.

Art glanced over at Camille.

"So what do you think they're going to do?"

Camille shook her head. "I don't know," she said. "But it won't be good. Did you see my mom? I haven't seen her this angry since the time I accidentally painted the cat blue."

"You did what?"

"Long story," said Camille.

Art paused. "I'm sorry I got you into this," he finally said.

"It's not your fault," Camille replied. "And it's like the woman said—no one even noticed what she was doing at the museum. But you did. That's pretty amazing."

"I should have told my father," Art said. "You tried to tell me, but I wouldn't listen. We wouldn't be in this mess if I hadn't been so stubborn."

Camille shrugged her shoulders. "I suppose, but you did what you thought was the right thing to do. Isn't that what grownups always tell us?"

Art nodded.

He had thought he was doing the right thing.

Except he had been doing exactly the wrong thing.

The door on the far side of the room creaked open. Art and Camille both turned toward it.

Art's father entered the room first, followed by Mary Sullivan, Catherine Dismuke, and—finally—Ludwig Hoggard III. Mr. Hoggard sat down in the seat directly across from Art and Camille. The other adults remained standing.

Mr. Hoggard looked at Art and Camille and then cleared his throat.

"Dr. Hamilton just informed me of your involvement

in the recent situation concerning the fake Van Gogh painting and the National Gallery of Art," Mr. Hoggard said. "And while it does not excuse what has occurred here this evening, it does condition my perspective on the matter.

"I love art," Mr. Hoggard continued. "It has been my family's passion for generations. And while I am troubled by your methods, I cannot fault your intent. You believed that you were protecting some of the most important works of art in the world."

Mr. Hoggard paused momentarily and looked directly at Art. "I hope I would have done the same at your age. I have conveyed my feelings to your father and have asked him to be lenient in whatever punishment he feels is appropriate."

He glanced at Camille. "And I have asked the same of your mother as well."

Art could not believe what he was hearing. The emotions that had been welling up inside him burst forth all at once, and the tears started streaming down his face. Camille reached over and put her arm around his shoulders. The room grew silent, and Art realized that everyone was now staring at him. He wiped the tears from his eyes and composed himself.

"I'm really sorry," he said to Mr. Hoggard. "I . . . didn't think enough about what I was doing."

Mr. Hoggard reached over and patted Art on the knee.

"Water under the bridge as far as I am concerned. But I'm afraid your parents may have other thoughts."

"I think you're right," said Camille.

"I know he's right," said Mary Sullivan from across the room.

CHAPTER 41

4:35 p.m.
Wednesday, April 20
Hamilton residence, Washington, DC

Art put his book down on the nightstand, stood up, and stretched. He had been reading ever since he got home from school, and it felt as if he had barely made a dent in the thick book.

His phone *pinged*. It was a text from Camille.

"Ugh," it read.

Art typed out a quick response. "Don't complain," he wrote. "It could have been a lot worse."

He hit Send. A moment later Camille responded.

"Still ugh," she wrote. "Grognard."

Art smiled. *Grognard* had become Camille's new favorite word to use. It had become her shorthand way of complaining about anything.

If she didn't like what she'd had for dinner? Grognard.

If she had to go to bed early? Grognard.

If she wanted to complain about their punishment? Grognard.

But Art also knew that he was right. Their punishments

could have been a lot worse. So Camille could grognard all she wanted.

After leaving the Wharf on Sunday night, they had traveled back home in complete silence. The quiet had been terrible, and Camille had squirmed in the seat beside him the whole trip. The taxi had dropped them off midway between Camille's house and Art's house—a short walk to either residence. Art's father and Mary Sullivan had conferred briefly on the sidewalk and then announced the punishments that would be implemented.

Both Art and Camille would be required to write letters of apology to both Mr. Hoggard and Ms. Dismuke. Not emails. Not text messages. Not some Word document typed out on a computer and printed. Not some simple "I'm sorry." They had to write the letters by hand on nice stationery, which they would then carefully fold and place into real envelopes to be mailed. Mary Sullivan said that writing a letter by hand was a sign of respect. Art's father had wholeheartedly agreed.

Art and Camille would also both be required to report home immediately after school for the rest of the year. No more trips to Starbucks. No more browsing through the comic book store on the way home. No more visits to the National Portrait Gallery to see Art's dad after school. No more hanging out at each other's houses watching television or playing video games. It would be straight home every day to work on the final bit of their punishment: book reports.

Both Art and Camille would be required to write a ten-page, single-spaced book report. On Monday morning Mary Sullivan had delivered their books. Camille had been assigned *The Count of Monte Cristo* by Alexandre Dumas—all 1,276 pages of it. Art had been assigned *Ulysses* by James Joyce, a far shorter but far more difficult book to read. Mary Sullivan had simply laughed when Camille asked if she could switch books with Art.

"Go ahead," her mother had said.

Apparently sensing her mother's delight in her suggestion, Camille had wisely decided to stick with the longer novel.

There were, of course, the deep expressions of disappointment in what Camille and Art had done. As far as Art was concerned, that was actually the worst part of the punishment. The guilt and embarrassment ate at him. It took two full days before he could look his father in the eyes.

The letter of apology had actually been enlightening for Art. He had initially started by trying to explain why he had thought that the museum was going to be robbed—but the more he wrote, the sillier it sounded. Why had he jumped to the conclusion that there was some grand conspiracy to rob the museum? How could he have thought that this had anything to do with the Gardner Museum theft? It all seemed so ridiculous in retrospect. He ended up taking his explanations out of the letter. He realized that he needed to apologize for what he did, not try to justify it.

The one punishment that was not implemented—but that was strongly considered—was not allowing Art and Camille to attend the gala for the Millennium Exhibit. Camille had burst into tears when her mother mentioned that as a possibility. However, both Art's father and Mary Sullivan had ultimately decided that the gala was a once-in-a-lifetime opportunity that the two simply could not miss. But there was one major caveat—Art and Camille would no longer be able to sit at one of the head tables. Art's father had felt that it would be disrespectful to seat Art and Camille anywhere near Mr. Hoggard, seeing as how they had just spied on him and accused him of planning to rob the museum. Art found it difficult to argue with his father's logic. They would therefore be relegated to a table in the back of the courtyard—close enough to enjoy the festivities but far enough away to avoid direct contact with the gala's main sponsor. Camille—in a text to Art—had referred to this as being seated at the kiddie table. She may have been right, but the alternative could have been a lot worse—they could be sitting at home eating pizza the night of the gala.

Art sat back down on his bed and grabbed *Ulysses* from the nightstand.

Why couldn't his father have assigned something from Erik Larson? he thought. At least that would have been entertaining—and educational as well.

Art opened the book and continued reading.

Grognard.

CHAPTER 42

5:35 p.m.
Saturday, April 23
Washington, DC

Art and his father made their way down the street toward the Sullivan residence. Art had worn a tuxedo on only one prior occasion—a black-tie function in Paris for an event at the Louvre when he was only nine years old.

He remembered feeling very self-conscious the entire night—like some little penguin waddling around while all the adults oohed and aahed over how cute he was.

He'd hated that.

But tonight felt different. He was tall enough to wear a men's tuxedo, not some stripped-down version made for little kids. And he had insisted on wearing a straight black tie and cummerbund instead of the usual bow tie. His father had initially resisted this break with tradition, but upon seeing Art in the full ensemble, he had admitted that it looked great.

The day had been a bit cooler than normal—a slight reminder that winter was not quite ready to let go—but otherwise the weather was perfect for the gala. There wasn't a cloud in the sky, and there was no chance of rain. His father had spent the past week working on all the final preparations for the Millennium Exhibit—checking and double-checking all of his instruments to make sure everything was working perfectly. Art, of course, had spent the entire week at home reading. He would have loved to have been there at the museum—there was a certain buzz of excitement leading up to an event like the Millennium Exhibit. Everyone was slightly on edge and giddy with excitement. And Art had missed it all.

It had been a rough week, but tonight was about to make up for it.

"Thanks for letting me go tonight," Art said to his father as they walked.

Arthur Hamilton Sr. put his arm around his son's shoulders. "I couldn't imagine going without you," he said. There was a slight hitch in his father's voice as he spoke. Art knew this past week had not been easy for his father, either. They had always done everything together.

"How's the book coming along?" his father asked.

"Have you ever actually read *Ulysses*?" Art replied.

"I tried once," his father said, "but I'm a bit more partial to scientific journals—chemical equations are easier to understand than James Joyce."

"Well, I'm sure it's good for me," Art replied.

Arthur Hamilton Sr. laughed. "Well, maybe you can explain it to me when you're done."

Art spotted Camille and her mother waiting for them outside the Sullivan home. Art waved and Camille immediately sprinted toward them.

"Don't mess up your dress!" Mary Sullivan yelled. "Or your hair!"

"Hey, Dr. Hamilton! Hey, Art!" Camille exclaimed as she came to a screeching halt in front of them and performed a curtsy. "I've been practicing—just in case I get to meet the queen."

"That was absolutely perfect," Art's father said. "And you look lovely this evening."

"I still hate dresses," Camille said. "But thanks."

Art agreed with his father. Camille looked great, although it was odd seeing her so dressed up—her normal ensemble usually involved jeans, T-shirts, and tennis shoes. She wore a red dress, a dark red sash, and red shoes—and her hair had been pulled behind her head and braided. Art knew it was only a matter of time before her hair—which seemed to have a life of its own—worked its way out of the knot into which it had been weaved. He imagined this happening with some sort of *Looney Tunes* sound effect accompanying it.

Mary Sullivan finally caught up with her daughter. "The car should be here in a couple of minutes," she said. "Everybody ready?"

Camille gave a thumbs-up. "I can't wait," she said. "What do you think the queen's like?" she asked. "I mean, I bet she's nice. I read she was a car mechanic during World War II—is that true? If it is, that is so cool. I would never think of a queen working on a car, but you never know. I wonder what she does now for fun. Wouldn't it be strange if she still . . ."

Art listened as Camille regaled them with her soliloquy about the queen. A car would be arriving any minute to whisk them off to the fanciest event he had ever attended—and the most important. He knew he had made some mistakes over the past week and a half. He had embarrassed his father. He had insulted the man who was sponsoring the Millennium Exhibit. He had stalked a world-renowned security expert. He had let his imagination get the better of him, and he had gotten his best friend into a whole lot of trouble. But standing there on the sidewalk with his father, Camille, and Mary Sullivan, everything seemed perfect.

CHAPTER 43

6:07 p.m.

Saturday, April 23

National Portrait Gallery, Washington, DC

The car dropped them off a block from the museum. A banner hanging from a nearby lamppost announced the opening of the Millennium Exhibit—but a banner was not necessary to understand that something important was taking place at the museum that evening. The roadway in front of the north entrance was blocked off—police officers and barriers kept any curious pedestrians at bay—and the entire front of the museum was lit with bright spotlights. Large black cars, limousines, and television trucks lined the street along the east side of the museum. Men dressed in tuxedos and women dressed in long gowns made their way up the steps to the north entrance. Art, his father, Camille, and Mary Sullivan joined the line of people entering the museum. They passed through the metal detectors that been installed in the north lobby, checked their names off the guest list, and stepped into the courtyard.

"Wow!" Camille exclaimed. "It's beautiful!"

Camille was right. The courtyard—which was incredible under normal circumstances—had been transformed into one of the most spectacular settings that Art had ever seen. The main stage had been set up at the west end of the courtyard—the backdrop behind the stage was the stone façade of the west wall. Images of the paintings in the Millennium Exhibit were being projected one by one onto the façade—the portrait of William Shakespeare, a Fayum mummy portrait, and works by Rembrandt van Rijn, Johannes Vermeer, James McNeill Whistler, Edgar Degas, Mary Cassatt, and Diego Rivera.

The images continued—Vincent van Gogh, Francisco Goya, Katsushika Hokusai, Frédéric Bazille, Edvard Munch, Édouard Manet, and Amy Sherald. The images filled the massive wall, transforming it into a giant, constantly evolving work of art.

The remaining walls of the courtyard were illuminated by amber-colored lights from above. Round tables with champagne-colored tablecloths filled the room, each accented with a flickering white candle. The courtyard's trees—lit from below—glowed bright green. A band played on a small stage next to the door leading to the south lobby while people mingled throughout the room. The wait staff—dressed head to toe in black—maneuvered around the room carrying trays of appetizers and drinks. And above them all, the clear night sky twinkled through the glass expanse that covered the courtyard. It was all quite magical.

Arthur Hamilton Sr. handed Art a small card with the number thirty-three printed on it. "This is the number for the table where you and Camille will be seated for dinner," he said. "Mary and I will be at the head table. If you need me, just text, okay?"

Art nodded. "Got it."

Mary Sullivan and Art's father headed toward their seats, which were located at the very front of the room next to the stage. Art pointed to his left—toward the opposite side of the courtyard.

"And we are that way," he said to Camille.

Camille sighed. "The kiddie table."

"Yep," Art replied. "The kiddie table."

"Grognard," Camille said.

Each table had a small metal stand that held a card with a number printed on it. They passed table fifteen, table eighteen, table twenty-one.

"Oh, c'mon," Camille muttered as they moved farther and farther away from the main stage.

They continued past table twenty-four, table twenty-seven, and table thirty until they reached the final row and the final table: table thirty-three.

"You have got to be kidding!" Camille exclaimed. She turned and looked across the full expanse of the courtyard.

"It must be a mile to the stage," she said.

"Just be happy that we're here," Art said. "We could be sitting at home reading."

"I am happy," Camille said as she plopped down into one of the seats at the table, "but nobody told me that I'd be sitting this far away."

Art certainly understood Camille's frustration—it would have been great to sit at the front table. They would have been in the middle of everything—only a few feet away from the queen once she arrived. And the front tables were loaded with all sorts of famous people—politicians, writers, artists, and at least one actress that Art recognized. He would have loved to have simply sat there and listened to those conversations. But it wasn't to be—and he had accepted that.

"Yeah," Art said. "It would be cool to be close, but how many people can say they've actually had dinner with the queen—even if we are on the other side of the room?"

Camille smiled. "Nobody that I know."

CHAPTER 44

6:23 p.m.

Saturday, April 23

National Portrait Gallery, Washington, DC

The room had started to fill up, and the guests were making their way toward their tables. A young couple had joined Art and Camille at table thirty-three, but after a brief introduction they had spent the rest of the time taking selfies and comparing the gala to all the other fancy events they had attended. Art didn't really mind that the young couple was ignoring him and Camille—he wasn't really in the mood for small talk with strangers. He preferred to sit back and take it all in—the people, the music, the decorations, and the ambience. The gala was like something out of a movie—it bordered on the unreal. And being in a tuxedo made it all the better, as though he were some sort of spy or something.

"Well, I finally figured it out," Camille said.

"Figured what out?"

"I figured out what *grognard* actually means," Camille said.

"I thought you had decided that it means 'this stinks,'" Art replied.

"Well, that's my definition," Camille replied. "But it's actually French. It means 'grumbler.' I'm surprised you didn't know—I thought you spoke French."

Art spoke fluent French, but he had never heard the word *grognard* before. And considering he had never used the word *grumbler* when speaking English, it sort of made sense. It wasn't exactly the kind of word that a person used on a regular basis—if at all.

"Sounds sort of old-fashioned," Art said. "There are a lot of French words like that—words that people don't really use anymore."

Art spotted his father and Ms. Sullivan sitting at the table next to the main stage. They were engaged in conversation with Mr. Hoggard and Ms. Dismuke, as well as an older couple that Art did not recognize.

"You're right," Camille said. "It had something to do with . . ."

The band continued to play as more people filtered into the courtyard. Art scanned the room for any sign of the actress he'd already spotted or any other famous person.

". . . long time ago in . . ." Camille continued.

Art had lost track of exactly what Camille was talking about—he just nodded every now and then to act as though he were listening. Besides, between the music and the conversations going on all across the room, it was becoming more and more difficult to hear anything.

". . . regiment that was based . . ." Camille droned on.

He spotted a few familiar faces in the crowd—mostly his father's staff from the conservation center. He could see the director of the museum anxiously pacing back and forth next to the stage. Art checked his watch—the queen would be arriving in about twenty minutes. He wondered what type of music the band would play when she arrived.

". . . Napoleon's guard or something like . . ." Camille continued.

Napoleon's guard?

"What did you just say?" Art asked.

"I said a grumbler was some sort of guard for that guy Napoleon from France," Camille replied. "It's what some of his guards were called—*grognards*—because they complained a lot. You know, grumblers."

Art felt as if he had been hit with a brick—he couldn't believe what he was hearing. He pulled out his phone and quickly Googled the words *Napoleon* and *grognard*.

He stared at the results of his search in disbelief. It couldn't be a coincidence.

He turned to Camille. He tried to speak, but the words wouldn't come out. His mouth was completely dry, and his heart was pounding a mile a minute. The room felt as if it were spinning around him.

"What's the matter?" Camille asked. "Are you sick? Did you eat one of the scallop thingies they were bringing around? I should have told you not to eat those."

Art took a deep breath to try to calm himself.

"I was right," he whispered to Camille. His voice cracked as he spoke.

"Right?" Camille asked. "Right about what?"

"There *is* a plot to steal the paintings," Art said, "and it's happening right now."

CHAPTER 45

6:26 p.m.

Saturday, April 23

National Portrait Gallery, Washington, DC

Camille's jaw dropped open. All she could do was stare at Art.

"I don't have time to explain," Art said, "but I've got to stop them from stealing the paintings."

Camille threw her hands up. "No, no, no, no."

All Camille wanted to do was see the Queen of England. That was it. A nice dinner and *see the queen.* Maybe some cheesecake for dessert. She had even been willing to wear a dress and get a braid put in her hair. She didn't have time to get dragged back into Art's crazy conspiracy.

"Don't worry," Art said, reading her mind. "You don't have to do anything—I've got this."

Camille leaned over and grabbed Art by the hand. "We were wrong," she said. "Don't do this. You will get in so much trouble."

"Five minutes," Art said. "Just give me five minutes. I just need to be sure. I *have* to be sure. If I'm wrong, then I'll be back before the queen even arrives."

Camille knew there was no way she was talking Art

out of whatever he was planning to do. "You *better* be back here in five minutes," she said. "I'm not reading another thousand-page book."

Camille watched as Art headed toward the tall cloth screens that had been put in place to hide the service area—the place where the food was kept before dinner was served. Camille knew exactly where Art was going—behind the screens was the door leading into the east wing of the museum. He was going to try to get to the gallery in which the Millennium Exhibit was located on the second floor.

You have to help him, a little voice inside her head said.

Camille told the little voice to shut up and mind its own business.

She didn't even know why Art had suddenly become convinced that he had been right all along. It clearly had something to do with the word *grognard,* but exactly what remained unclear. She wanted to kick herself for even mentioning it.

I'm staying right here, she told herself. If Art wanted to spend the rest of his life doing book reports as punishment, then let him.

Camille turned away from the back of the room and tried to focus on what was happening on the stage. A young woman in a black dress was adjusting the microphone on the podium. She seemed to be having a hard time getting the microphone to stay in place.

But what if something happens? the little voice asked. *What if he needs help?*

The little voice was annoying.

Camille turned her attention to the band by the south entrance. They were playing a nice jazzy tune. It sounded familiar, but she had no idea what the song was called. Art would probably have known.

Seriously, the little voice said, *he didn't even know how to use a scooter.*

I told you to shut up, Camille answered back.

And he had no plan for getting into the fourth floor of the office building.

Honestly, Camille wondered angrily, *don't you have something better to do?*

He didn't know what DCYC meant. And the drone? Your brilliant friend didn't think of the drone, you did. What was his plan for getting to the yacht? Nothing. He had no plan.

He's your best friend, the little voice said.

Crud, Camille thought.

Not surprisingly, no one was paying attention to the twelve-year-old in a tuxedo. The wait staff and chefs were scurrying around getting ready for the first course—a long table lined with plates of salad stood at the ready. Art made his way around the perimeter of the service area and scooted along the interior wall of the courtyard until he had reached the doors leading into the east wing of the museum.

He glanced through the doors. A row of catering carts was lined up against the wall, filled with large insulated plastic containers designed to keep food hot until it was ready to be served. Two young men were unloading more carts from the elevator in the hallway. Otherwise, everything seemed clear. There was no sign of any security guards. Art started to reach for the door when a hand suddenly clamped down on his shoulder. His heart jumped in his chest.

"I'm sorry," he muttered, "I was just—"

"Just being stupid," Camille interrupted. "Honestly, did you think you could actually do this without me?"

Art turned to face his friend. "I don't want to get you into more trouble."

"You should have thought of that a week ago," Camille replied. "And besides, you're not the boss of me. So what's the plan?"

Art sighed. He knew one absolute truth about his diminutive, red-haired friend—there was no sense in trying to talk her out of doing anything she had set her mind to.

"We're going to check out the Millennium Exhibit," he said. "If what I think is happening is happening, I'll text my dad. That's it. No hero stuff."

"And if nothing's wrong?"

"Then we're back in our seats in five minutes," Art replied.

Camille smiled. "Deal."

CHAPTER 46

6:28 p.m.

Saturday, April 23

National Portrait Gallery, Washington, DC

Art opened the door, stepped inside the hallway, and pulled the door shut behind them. The two young men unloading the catering carts from the elevator glanced up at them, shrugged, and continued about their business.

"So how do we get there?" Camille asked.

Good question, thought Art. The Millennium Exhibit was located on the second floor on the opposite side of the building. Making their way around the inside of the museum seemed risky—there were bound to be security guards and video cameras. Fortunately, there was a more direct route.

"The basement," Art replied. They could take the stairs down to the basement, go directly under the courtyard, and then take the stairs on the other side of the building straight up to the second floor. It would be best to avoid the elevators—elevators made a lot of noise, and Art knew they needed to be as quiet as possible.

The young men had unloaded the carts from the elevator and were now moving them into place at the far end of the hallway. Art and Camille took the opportunity to make their way over to a doorway on the opposite wall. The sign read AUTHORIZED PERSONNEL ONLY. Art pushed the door open, and they stepped inside the stairwell.

The stairways on the top three floors of the National Portrait Gallery were works of art—wide sweeping designs of marble, bronze, and wood. They were beautiful. They were graceful. The stairs leading to the basement of the museum, not so much. The stairs in the east wing were concrete, painted a dull gray, and scuffed with use. The railing was made of steel and free of any discernible artistry. Camille and Art stood at the top of the stairs and stared down over the railing. There was no one in sight.

"Ready?" Camille asked.

"Almost," Art replied. He pointed at his feet. "Shoes," he said. "We need to ditch them. They'll be way too loud."

Camille nodded. Art was wearing a pair of black shoes with hard leather heels. Her flats were lined with leather soles. The two of them would sound like a pair of horses marching on concrete if they started walking around like that. They removed their shoes and placed them against the wall.

Making their way quickly and quietly down the stairs

to the basement below, they paused briefly. The door at the bottom of the stairs once again warned that access was limited to authorized personnel only.

Art cracked open the door and peeked into the basement corridor. The passageway was wide—almost thirty feet across—and was filled with row after row of the same catering carts that filled the hallway above. Again, there was no one in sight.

"Let's go," Art said.

They stepped into the corridor. Camille considered the long passageway every bit as charming as the stairs leading down to it. The walls were brick and the ceiling was concrete. Thick black pipes ran along the ceiling down the length of the corridor. The air was thick and musty. Fluorescent lights provided a bright, unnatural glow to the space. It was hard to believe this was part of the same grand and beautiful building that sat directly above it.

Art and Camille passed cart after cart, each labeled with a description of its contents: CHICKEN, STEAK, AU GRATIN POTATOES, BREAD, ASPARAGUS, BUTTER, CRÈME BRÛLÉE, FRESH FRUIT. Carts were filled with large containers of tea and stacked high with bottles of sparkling water. Camille was amazed at the volume of food needed to feed everyone at the gala. She also noted that there were no carts labeled CHEESECAKE. That was disappointing.

To their right was the service elevator and a door leading to the loading dock. Camille knew that the two young men would be back down in short order to get more carts. She and Art needed to move quickly.

Art led the way down the corridor. Once they had made it past the last row of carts, he indicated that they were probably halfway across the courtyard.

"Just a bit farther," he said.

They passed doors labeled MAINTENANCE, FACILITIES, STORAGE, SUPPLIES, and FIRE SUPPRESSION. They passed a large set of double doors with a sign that identified the entrance as the MECHANICAL ROOM—the room hummed loudly and the floor outside trembled ever so slightly.

Camille heard the *bing* of the elevator behind them in the corridor. The elevator doors would be opening soon. They would no longer be alone.

Art also heard it.

"We need to hurry," he urged.

Their feet made a soft tapping sound as they ran down the corridor. Camille could feel her heart pounding in her chest. Art reached the end of the corridor first—he turned the corner, sliding sideways in his socks before recovering and slipping out of view. Camille followed close behind. They stood with their backs against the basement wall. It had not been a very long run, but Camille found herself panting and out of breath.

Calm down, she told herself.

She glanced over at Art. He pointed at the set of stairs to their left. The stairs were different from the steps at the other end of the corridor—they were more elaborate, like the rest of the museum. Art had explained that the west wing stairs were older—part of the museum's original construction.

"Ready?" Art asked.

Camille nodded. "Ready."

CHAPTER 47

6:32 p.m.

Saturday, April 23

National Portrait Gallery, Washington, DC

The stairs were dark—the ornate bronze lanterns that lined the exterior wall of the stairs had been turned off for the night.

"Well, that's not the least bit scary," Camille whispered.

Art had to suppress a laugh. She was right—the setting certainly matched the circumstances. They were dressed in formal evening clothes—a tuxedo, for goodness' sake—as if they were in some sort of spy movie or a video game, and they were about to ascend a grand staircase to try to stop the theft of a billion dollars' worth of art.

But it wasn't a movie. Or a video game.

This was very real.

Art closed his eyes and listened for any sounds from the shadows above. He could just make out the faint strains of the band playing in the courtyard, but that was it. He gave a thumbs-up and they started climbing the stairs.

They made it to the first landing, between the basement and the first floor. All of Art's nerve endings seemed to be on high alert—he felt as if an electrical current were running through his entire body. He told himself to be patient, not to rush. He paused and listened once more. All seemed normal—just the sounds of the band.

They continued up toward the first floor landing. Art stopped just short of the landing and peeked around the corner. It was empty—and dark. They stepped onto the landing, quickly turned the corner, and headed up the next set of stairs toward the second floor.

They paused once more at the next landing. Art stood against the cold stone wall of the stairway and closed his eyes. The music from the courtyard had grown louder, and he could now hear the murmur of voices from the guests milling about the room. But that was it. No footsteps. No voices on the landing above them.

They were close. The hallway leading to the Millennium Exhibit was at the top of the stairs. Art pulled out his phone. If he was correct—if thieves were trying to steal the paintings—he would immediately notify his father. He had promised Camille that they wouldn't try to be heroes. Just observe and report. That was it.

Art took a deep breath.

It was time to go.

Art and Camille started up the stairs. They had made it halfway when—suddenly—a dark figure appeared in front of them on the landing.

"You shouldn't be here," a man's voice announced from the top of the stairs.

Camille froze in place.

Part of her wanted to turn around and run away, but she could see the silhouette of a walkie-talkie in the man's hand. With one call, the stairs and basement would be swarming with security. Her mind raced through a million different scenarios—but each scenario ended with her getting in even more trouble than she would already be. They were busted, and there was nothing they could do about it.

"Come up here," the silhouetted figure at the top of the stairs ordered.

Camille glanced over at Art. He nodded. The look on his face said it all: they had failed.

CHAPTER 48

6:33 p.m.

Saturday, April 23

National Portrait Gallery, Washington, DC

They were starting up the stairs when the voice spoke again.

"Arthur?" the voice said. "Camille?"

The voice was now softer—friendlier. Camille recognized it instantly.

"Phil!" she exclaimed.

She and Art made it to the top of the stairs and found themselves standing in front of the elderly security guard. He seemed as astonished as they were to be staring at one another.

"You scared the dickens out of me," he said.

He pointed to a chair on the far side of the landing—right next to the window facing out to the courtyard. "I was just sitting here listening to the band play when I heard you," he said. "My heart nearly jumped out of my chest."

"We're sorry," Art replied. "We didn't mean to scare you."

Phil's face was pale—he seemed genuinely shaken by their sudden appearance.

"I'll be fine," Phil assured them. "I just wasn't expecting any excitement this evening—I mean, other than seeing the Queen of England. Now, that will be pretty exciting, but not the same type of excitement as getting almost scared to death. You know, there was this one time that I swear I saw the queen at this Applebee's out in Maryland. She was eating all-you-can-eat ribs. My friend Bob—he was with me—he said, 'That's not the queen,' but I said—"

Phil paused.

"Hey—what exactly are you two doing up here anyway?" he asked. "I was told this area was off-limits to guests. Did your dad send you?"

Camille glanced over at Art. She could practically see the wheels turning in his head.

What now? she wondered.

They were fewer than twenty-five feet from the doorway leading into the Millennium Exhibit—just a short walk down the hallway to their left.

There was, Art realized, only one thing to do.

Tell the truth.

"I think someone's trying to rob the museum," Art said.

The words lingered in the air. Camille's head snapped around, and she stared directly at Art as if she couldn't believe what he had just said.

Camille wasn't the only one surprised. Phil's eyes went wide, his jaw dropped open, and his mustache started twitching. His glasses nearly fell off the end of his nose.

"A r-robbery?" Phil stammered. "You're kidding, right? You're just joshing ol' Phil. That's what it is—just a joke, right?"

Art shook his head. "I'm not joking. It's a long story, but I'm not joking."

Phil looked at Camille, who had finally recovered from her initial shock. "He's not kidding," she assured him.

"But how could they?" Phil asked. "No one could get into that room without setting off all sorts of alarms. And I've been sitting here for almost an hour—I haven't heard a thing."

"They know all about the security," Art said. "I don't have time to explain how, but they know all about the cameras, the motion detectors, the rotation of the security guards—all of it. They probably know you're sitting out here right now. They just need a few minutes to pull this off, and they've probably already hacked into the security system and taken it over. I bet everything looks perfectly normal from the security office—but I don't think it is."

Art pointed toward the set of double doors at the far end of the hallway.

"I think the thieves are already in the gallery," Art said.

"And they are preparing to steal some of the most famous paintings in the world."

Phil's face—which had already been pale—was now practically white. "We . . . we need to call . . . someone," he muttered as he started to reach for the walkie-talkie on his belt.

Art reached over and placed his hand on the elderly guard's arm.

"Not yet," Art said.

"Not yet?" Phil exclaimed. "But . . . but . . . what if . . . they steal all the paintings? I will be in so much trouble, and I really like this job."

Phil was clearly shaken. Art knew he needed to get the situation under control before it got out of hand.

"Let's just check it out first," Art said. "Just a quick peek. We don't want to cause a big fuss if I'm wrong, do we?"

Art could see Phil starting to come around. "It would be a pretty big fuss," Phil conceded.

"A huge fuss," Camille added. "And besides, Art's probably wrong—there's no way anyone could get into that room. So before you start calling for help, why don't we just check it out. You know, just to be sure."

Phil nodded. Some of the color appeared to have returned to his face. He took a deep breath. "I think that would be best," he said. "Just to be sure."

* * *

They huddled together at the top of the stairs. Camille and Phil looked at Art.

"So what's the plan?" Phil asked.

Art turned and glanced down the hallway toward the doors leading into the exhibit. If he was wrong about the theft, security would immediately be alerted as soon as they stepped into the room. Everyone—including his father and Camille's mother—would know they were there.

Art smiled. He had not planned on running into Phil, but maybe Art could turn this to his advantage. A couple of kids stepping into the exhibit would cause all sorts of problems, but what about a security guard?

"We need you to check it out," Art said.

"Me?" Phil asked. "Listen, all I do is keep people from touching the paintings and stuff like that. What if there really are bad guys in there? What am I supposed to do?"

"Nothing," replied Art. "You just poke your head into the room—that's all. If there's nothing going on, then fine. Tell the security people you heard something and went to check. They'll believe you. But if you see something, we alert everyone."

"I don't know," Phil said. "It seems sort of risky."

"You'd be a hero," Camille added.

Phil's eyebrows went up. Camille had obviously hit on something. "Do you really think so?"

"Absolutely," Art replied. "Your name would be all over the news."

"And my photo?" Phil asked.

"And your photo," Camille replied.

Phil nodded. "I'll do it."

Art glanced over at Camille and smiled.

Were things finally going their way?

CHAPTER 49

6:35 p.m.

Saturday, April 23

National Portrait Gallery, Washington, DC

They made their way down the short hallway to the set of double doors leading into the Millennium Exhibit. The hallway was dark and cool, and music continued to play behind them in the courtyard. Art checked the time on his phone. The queen was scheduled to arrive in fewer than ten minutes.

Art wasn't quite sure how he felt. What if he was right? What if there were thieves on the other side of the doors? Things could still go wrong even if they alerted security. It could still be a very dangerous situation. Maybe, Art thought, it would be better if he was wrong—if there was nothing on the other side of the doors other than a gallery filled with famous portraits. It wouldn't be so bad if he was wrong.

They now stood just a few feet from the doors. Art listened intently for any sounds from within the room, but the music and noise from the courtyard made it difficult to hear. If something was going on inside the room, there was only one way to find out.

"Ready?" Art whispered to Phil.

The older gentleman nodded and gave a thumbs-up. "Ready."

Phil edged forward toward the door on the right. He reached out, grabbed the handle, and then . . . nothing.

He's scared, Art thought.

Art was not necessarily surprised. Phil's job usually involved keeping inquisitive school kids from getting too close to the paintings in the museum and giving directions to tourists incapable of reading a museum map. Stopping a bunch of professional thieves was probably not something he had ever expected to do.

The older gentleman took a deep breath and turned to face Camille and Art. He removed his glasses and stuck them into his shirt pocket.

"I'm sorry," Phil said. "I really am."

Camille noticed it as soon as he turned around.

It may have been the slight change in the tone of his voice—it was now deeper and a bit more confident.

Or perhaps it was the way he now stood—taller, less stooped over.

Or perhaps it was his eyes. The kind, gentle eyes were

gone. With the glasses removed, he now seemed far more intense, his eyes narrowed and focused.

The transformation was subtle but clear.

Camille gasped.

I think we're in trouble.

The smile on Phil's face said it all, but the gun pointed at them confirmed it.

"I'm impressed," Phil said. "But I'm afraid your little investigation has come to an end."

Art couldn't find the words to respond. Just a few moments ago he had been speaking to an elderly security guard whom he had known since his father started working at the museum. And now Art was staring at a man who seemed to be at least twenty years younger and two inches taller. The transformation was incredible.

Phil—or whatever his name may have been—reached over and grabbed the door's handle. He opened the door and motioned with his gun for Art and Camille to step inside the gallery.

They entered the gallery, and Phil pulled the door shut behind them.

Camille gasped again.

Two men stood in the middle of the room. They were

dressed as caterers—the same head-to-toe black outfits as the rest of the wait staff. There were, of course, a couple of differences. These two men wore gloves and had tool belts around their waists. And they were also carrying a large painting. Camille recognized it as the painting by Mary Cassatt. Cassatt was an Impressionist—one of the very few women who had become famous in a movement dominated by men such as Monet, Degas, and Renoir.

Camille had always liked this painting by Cassatt. It wasn't a formal portrait with everyone carefully posed for the artist. It was more like a photograph—a quick moment in time captured by the artist.

The two men stood and stared at Phil, obviously waiting for some sort of explanation.

"We've had a bit of a complication," Phil said, "but the timeline remains the same."

The two men nodded and then proceeded to load the painting into one of the large catering carts Art and Camille had seen in the basement.

"And where did we put that duct tape?" Phil asked.

CHAPTER 50

6:39 p.m.

Saturday, April 23

National Portrait Gallery, Washington, DC

He could hear the band playing in the courtyard and the murmur of hundreds of voices as everyone anxiously waited for the queen's arrival. His father and Mary Sullivan were likely sitting at a table fewer than a hundred feet away. And just a few feet behind them was a window that faced out to Ninth Street—a street absolutely packed with police officers and security. That was what made it so infuriating to Art. They were so close and yet incapable of doing anything to prevent what was taking place right in front of their eyes.

Art sat on the carpeted floor beside Camille, their shoulders touching. His hands had been bound behind his back and a piece of duct tape placed over his mouth. He glanced over at Camille—she had likewise been tied up and silenced. They had been placed against a wall in the middle of the room—a vantage point from which they could be seen at all times by the three men. Their phones had been taken from them, and they were at least fifty feet from the nearest exit. There was no chance of escaping or warning anyone. Even if their mouths had not been taped shut, they could have screamed their heads off and stomped their feet all they wanted—no one in the courtyard below would have heard them.

Art glanced over at Camille. Her eyes were tinged with red—she was doing her best to keep from crying. It *was* a scary and uncertain situation. She looked at him, and they made eye contact. It was the best he could do under the circumstances.

The two men in the catering outfits moved swiftly and precisely around the room. Their training had clearly paid off—one masterpiece after another was being removed from the walls with ruthless efficiency. They were incredibly silent as they went about their work, and there was no wasted movement. Phil—or whoever he was—stood on the far side of the room. He appeared to be monitoring something on an iPad—Art suspected that it was the live security video of the corridors leading to the exhibit.

"Queen arrives in six minutes," one of the men said. "Let's get this wrapped up."

So I was right, Art thought. They clearly intended to use the queen's arrival as the distraction they needed to escape. Everyone would be focused on the queen—the guards, the police, the media, the museum staff, and the guests. One of the most famous people in the entire world was about to walk through the front door of the National Portrait Gallery. No one—at that particular moment—would be giving a second thought to the exhibit itself. After all, why should they? According to all the fancy security equipment monitoring the room, everything was perfectly normal—just a bunch of really expensive paintings hanging on the walls.

"Five minutes," one of the men called out.

Only three paintings remained—the Degas, the Rembrandt, and the large painting hanging on the wall directly across from Art.

Art knew that most people would not know the painting by its formal title. It was most commonly referred to as simply *Whistler's Mother.* Painted in 1871, it showed the artist's elderly mother, seated in profile against a gray wall, wearing a black dress. As odd as it may seem now, it had been a controversial painting when it was first displayed—hated by many critics for the painter's use of such plain and austere colors. It was, after all, the Gilded Age, and works of art were expected to reflect the unbridled optimism of the era. But time served as the ultimate critic, and the painting had become one of the world's most beloved and recognizable paintings. It had appeared in advertisements, on a postage stamp, in cartoons, on television, on T-shirts, and even in the movies.

The painter, James McNeill Whistler, was born in the United States, but the artist and his art belonged to the world. Whistler spent much of his life abroad and ultimately died in England. And although the painting itself was owned by France, it was universally considered one of the most important American paintings in history. To say it was priceless would be a disservice. It was iconic. It was a measure of an age. It was what art was supposed to be.

And it was about to be stolen.

What had happened to the paintings that had been stolen from the Isabella Stewart Gardner Museum? They had disappeared forever. There had not been so much as a rumor as to the whereabouts of the Gardner paintings. They were simply gone. The Rembrandts were gone. The Vermeer was gone. The Degas drawings were gone. The Manet was gone.

It made Art furious. He had spent his entire life hanging around the most famous works of art in history. He understood the power of art. His father had once been asked to consult on an exhibit at the Museum of Fine Arts in Boston. It was early evening, and the museum had closed for the day. While his father worked with the museum staff, Art had wandered the halls of the museum. He soon found himself standing in a dark gallery, a single spotlight focused on a painting by Toulouse-Lautrec. Art knew all about Lautrec—a brilliant artist whose life had ended far too early. Lautrec had lived in Paris during the height of the Post-Impressionist movement, and his artwork captured the joy and tragedy of that period. The painting—a work of art on cardboard—was magical. It captured the life of a real person—it was as if Art were seeing Paris through the eyes of the tragic artist. That was what these men were stealing—a view of the world that would be lost forever.

The people who had planned this theft were smart, sophisticated, and professional. They had put all the pieces in place—even down to arranging for the specific works of art that they wanted to steal to be placed in one room. They had hijacked the entire security system and created the perfect distraction for them to simply walk away with a billion dollars' worth of art. The theft at the Isabella Stewart Gardner Museum would pale in comparison.

It was the perfect crime.

Almost.

As smart as the thieves may have been, they had not quite thought of everything.

CHAPTER 51

6:41 p.m.

Saturday, April 23

National Portrait Gallery, Washington, DC

Although his forearms and wrists were bound together behind his back, his hands remained free. Art ran his fingers across the baseboard on the wall behind him. It was—disappointingly—smooth. He would have to move a bit farther down the wall. But that presented a number of risks. He couldn't move too far too fast or the thieves would notice. And it would also require coordinating with Camille. They had been placed shoulder to shoulder on the floor—his plan wouldn't work if the thieves looked up to discover him a foot away from her.

Art waited until the thieves had turned their backs to him, then glanced over at Camille. He nodded at her to get her attention. He then blinked once, twice, and on the third blink, he scooted over to his right a couple of inches. The sudden movement caught Camille by surprise, and her eyes went wide. She leaned precariously to her right.

Art nodded at her once more and then motioned with his head for her to scoot over as well. Camille stared at him.

At this point he wasn't sure if she was paralyzed with fear or simply angry at him for getting her back into this mess. It really didn't matter under the circumstances—he just needed her to move. He glanced yet again at the thieves—they were now working to remove the Degas portrait from the wall, and their attention was turned completely to that task. He looked back over at Camille, nodded, and then motioned for her to scoot over.

There was a slight pause. Camille stared at him for a moment, nodded, and then scooted over until they were once more shoulder to shoulder.

What is Art doing? Camille wondered.

He was up to something. Exactly what that might be was unclear.

Her heart was thumping in her chest. She felt as if she might hyperventilate and pass out. She understood how bad the situation was for them. She had already run all the possible scenarios through her mind—none of which were good.

If she had not made that stupid comment about the name of that stupid boat, they wouldn't be in this mess. But no, she'd just had to go and say something. So instead they were tied up on the floor in the middle of the Millennium Exhibit while a trio of thieves stole a billion dollars' worth of art. And now Art had apparently decided—for whatever reasons he might have had—that he needed to move a couple of inches to his right. But that was good enough for her. She didn't need to know the reasons. At least they were doing something.

CHAPTER 52

6:42 p.m.

Saturday, April 23

National Portrait Gallery, Washington, DC

"Three minutes," one of the men announced.

Art and Camille were running out of time. The thieves had removed the Degas painting from its frame. Only two paintings remained.

Art felt once more behind his back, but the baseboard remained smooth and flat.

They would need to move again.

The thieves had started the process of removing the Rembrandt portrait. Their attention was once again diverted.

Art glanced at Camille and nodded. He then blinked once, twice, and on the third blink, he scooted another two inches to his right. This time Camille moved in unison.

Art moved his hands along the baseboard once more. Nothing. He twisted his torso to the left and stretched his hands as far as he could along the baseboard to his right. His left shoulder felt as if it would pop out of its socket at any moment. And that's when he felt it. It was just the edge, but it was there.

Yes!

They would need to move again but this time just to ensure that he was positioned perfectly. He looked at Camille, nodded, and blinked the countdown once more. They moved two inches. He nodded again and repeated the process. Two more inches.

He felt once more behind his back.

Perfect.

He had found her.

He had found their protector.

He had found Soteria.

CHAPTER 53

6:43 p.m.
Saturday, April 23
National Portrait Gallery, Washington, DC

Art ran his fingers over the small rectangular device attached to the baseboard behind his back. It was one of the hundreds of environmental monitoring devices his father had placed around the room—the Soteria, as his father had called them.

The protectors.

It had occurred to Art that the virtual reality training program used by the thieves to plan the heist had taken into consideration every part of the museum's extensive security system. They knew where every camera was located. They knew where every motion detector was located. They knew that every painting in the exhibit had sensors that alerted security if someone got too close to the painting or tried to remove it from the wall. They knew the precise rotation and timing of security guards throughout the building. They knew how to bypass all of the security. They knew how to override the video monitors—to show the security room exactly what the thieves wanted them to see, not what was actually happening.

But there was one thing that the training program had not considered—Art's father's environmental monitors. And why would they? The monitors were not attached to any of the paintings. The monitors didn't alert anyone if the paintings were stolen or if someone broke into the room. They were not part of the security system. The only thing the monitors did was continuously check the temperature, humidity, and air quality in the room. And unless something went terribly wrong, the system just did its job—automatically correcting the temperature in the room, adjusting the humidity, and maintaining the air quality.

It was time to make things go terribly wrong.

Art placed his right hand over the monitoring device and pressed as hard as he could against it. He needed to cover it completely. He needed to make it as hot as he could, as fast as he could. And a good dose of hand sweat wouldn't hurt either—it was filled with all sorts of interesting chemicals.

"Two minutes," Phil announced. The men had removed the Rembrandt and now turned to the Whistler painting.

C'mon, Soteria, Art urged. *Do your job.*

* * *

"Have you ever met the queen?" Mary Sullivan asked. She sat next to Arthur Hamilton Sr. at the head table in the courtyard. The museum's chief of security had just notified Dr. Hamilton that the queen would be arriving at the museum in fewer than two minutes. The news had spread fast and the entire room was buzzing in anticipation. Everyone was scrambling to find their seats.

Dr. Hamilton shook his head. "I've met a lot of royalty from a lot of countries," he said. "But this is a new one for me."

"Are you nervous?" Ms. Sullivan asked. "Because I've got to admit—my knees are shaking. I can't believe we will be sitting at the same table as the Queen of England."

Dr. Hamilton smiled. "My nerves are completely shot," he replied. "The only other time I've felt this nervous meeting someone was when—"

Dr. Hamilton was interrupted by a buzzing sound coming from his coat pocket. It was his phone.

"I bet it's Art," he said. "He hasn't said anything, but I know he's still pretty sore about getting stuck in the back of the room. He probably wants to know what's going on up here."

Dr. Hamilton retrieved the phone from his pocket. But it wasn't a text message or a phone call from Art.

It was Soteria.

One of the monitors in the exhibit hall was reporting a spike in temperature up to eighty degrees and an increase in humidity level by almost fifty percent. The monitor was also—strangely—showing the presence of ammonia in the air.

Dr. Hamilton quickly scrolled through the other monitors in the room, all of which seemed to be normal. Normal temperature. Normal humidity level. No sign of ammonia in the air. The problem appeared to be confined to a single device.

That's strange, Dr. Hamilton thought, *but not necessarily a concern.* He knew that the environmental system would automatically start making the necessary adjustments. In fact, the app on his phone indicated that the vent above the area in which the monitor was located had already been activated—fresh, cool air was already being blown into the room, and the moist air was being vented out. Filters in the system would quickly dispense of any ammonia in the area.

It was probably just a malfunction with the unit, Dr. Hamilton concluded. He made a mental note to check on it later that evening. He returned the phone to his pocket.

Problem solved, he thought. Modern technology was wonderful.

CHAPTER 54

6:44 p.m.

Saturday, April 23

National Portrait Gallery, Washington, DC

"One minute," Phil announced.

All of the paintings—a billion dollars' worth—had been removed from their frames and packed into two large catering carts. The exposed edges of the paintings were then covered with metal railing that made them look like large serving trays. Anyone glancing inside the carts would have no idea what was really inside. The tools the men had used to remove the paintings from the walls were placed in a hidden compartment below the artwork.

Art continued to press his hand as hard as he could against the monitoring device behind his back. He had known that his efforts were working when the vent above his head suddenly came on and started blowing cool air directly down onto him and Camille. But so far no one had shown up to check on the device.

The men conferred briefly, and then they made their way over to Art and Camille. Phil bent down directly in front of them and checked the bindings on their legs.

"I have to give it to you kids," Phil said. "What you did was pretty darn impressive. I don't know how you uncovered what we were doing, but it'll make a great story one day."

Phil patted Camille on the head.

"But seriously," he said, "did you really think I would fall for *frecklenosis?*"

Phil stood up, put his glasses back on, and stooped over ever so slightly. The old Phil had returned. The transformation was remarkable. Phil winked at them, turned, and walked away.

All Art could do was stare as Phil joined the other two men and they rolled the catering carts toward the exit and the service elevator leading to the basement. Moments later the men disappeared through the exit doors. As if on cue, the noise from the courtyard came to a sudden end and the room was silent. Camille glanced over at Art. He could see the hope in her eyes—the expectation that whatever Art had been doing had worked. But she was wrong. Art merely shook his head. He knew exactly what was about to happen. Suddenly, the strains of "God Save the Queen" started playing in the courtyard. Applause erupted.

Camille's eyes went wide with recognition.

The queen had arrived.

I failed, Art thought.

CHAPTER 55

6:45 p.m.

Saturday, April 23

National Portrait Gallery, Washington, DC

The elevator started its slow descent to the basement.

Phil checked the time on his watch—everything looked good.

He leaned against the catering carts and exhaled. It felt like the first time he had been able to catch his breath all evening.

"I'm getting too old for this," he said.

The two men dressed as caterers merely nodded. They had barely spoken a handful of words the entire evening. Even standing in the elevator they avoided direct eye contact. Phil didn't know their names or anything about them. He had met them for the first time this evening. They probably wore colored contacts, and their hair had almost certainly been dyed. Phil smiled. His eyes were actually green and his hair was dark brown with a long white streak across the front—far different from the mustached, blue-eyed, gray-haired guy who had been working security at the museum for the past year. Five hours from now he would be unrecognizable—as would the two men standing in the elevator with him.

A large white catering van waited for them in the basement garage. They would load up the carts and take the short drive south toward Arlington, Virginia, to a parking garage attached to a hotel on the outskirts of the city. They would park the catering van on the third floor of the parking garage, in the easternmost corner. The security cameras at the deck would be deactivated five minutes before their arrival. They would change out of the catering uniforms and the security guard outfit and then head off by foot in different directions. What happened to the contents of the catering van at that point was not his problem. Cars would be waiting for each of them at predesignated locations in Arlington. Phil knew where only his car was located—he knew nothing about where the other two men were headed or what type of vehicles were waiting there for them. Again, that was the plan—the less each of them knew, the better. Once they reached their vehicles, they would each send a text message to a different number—a number that would immediately be disconnected once the message was sent. However, the message would trigger the immediate deposit of five million dollars into each of their overseas accounts. They would then drive off in separate vehicles from separate locations to destinations unknown by anyone other than themselves. There was only one other condition—they could never return to Washington, DC.

The elevator reached the basement and came to a stop with a slight hitch and a bump. Phil glanced over at the caterers and nodded. No words were needed. They knew what to do—go straight to the catering van and pack up the carts. Phil, however, had another task. He had not been completely truthful with the kids. There was no way they could be left behind. They knew too much. He would retrieve an empty catering cart and return to get them. They would be left with the van in the parking deck in Arlington. He would leave it to others to decide their fate.

CHAPTER 56

6:47 p.m.

Saturday, April 23

National Portrait Gallery, Washington, DC

Art sat on the floor and stared out across the empty gallery. He could hear someone speaking from the stage and the occasional burst of applause in the courtyard below. The gala was proceeding forward—seemingly in complete denial of what had just happened. A billion dollars' worth of art had just walked out the door of the National Portrait Gallery. He glanced over at Camille. She still seemed to be in shock over what had occurred.

Just more than twenty minutes ago they had been sitting in the courtyard waiting for their salads to be served and for the queen to arrive. Now they were tied up with duct tape and left sitting against a wall. Art knew that the thieves could not leave them behind—he and Camille knew too much. The thieves had not said anything, but Art had seen the looks they had exchanged. It was only a matter of time before they returned to get the two of them. He didn't know if Camille had realized this or not—but they were running out of time.

Art took a deep breath and tried to assess the situation. He wiggled his legs, but the duct tape had been secured tightly from his ankles up to his thighs. He tried prying his arms apart. He could feel the edges of the tape cutting into his forearms and wrists. He could feel his fingers going numb, but the tape didn't budge.

There was only one chance. He would have to try to roll himself across the room. Maybe he could find some way to reach one of the exit doors and alert another guard—or something. Art wasn't quite sure what he would do, but he needed to do something. Sitting against the wall was not an option.

Art lay down on his side and stretched out. He was facing the doors leading into the hallway. He took a deep breath and rolled over. It was tougher than he thought it would be. He was now facing Camille. She just stared at him, her eyes wide. Again, Art wondered if she understood the nature of their situation as well as he did. By the look in her eyes, he suspected she did.

Art rolled over once again. He was now sweating profusely. The tape over his mouth made it difficult to breathe and to catch his breath.

He rolled again. And again. And again.

He was now starting to feel lightheaded. He couldn't seem to draw in enough air through his nose. But he couldn't stop.

He rolled again.

And again.

He had made it almost halfway across the floor. His back was to the doors, and he was facing Camille. The shocked look on her face had given way to what appeared to be an expression of hope.

And that's when he heard them.

The sounds were faint, but Art knew immediately what they were.

Footsteps.

The sounds were coming down the hallway from the elevator.

The thieves had returned.

The footsteps grew closer.

Art wanted to tell Camille how sorry he was for getting her into this mess.

The footsteps stopped. They had reached the doors.

Art looked at Camille.

He heard the creak of the door as it opened. Camille's eyes went wide.

But . . . something was different.

He could see it in her face. The fear was gone.

"Well, this was not how I expected this evening to go," a voice said from behind him.

His father's voice.

Art rolled over once more to see the room filling with

officers from the Metropolitan Police Department and security guards from the museum. Standing in the middle of them all was Arthur Hamilton Sr. and Mary Sullivan.

"Camille!" Mary Sullivan exclaimed, and rushed over.

Art's father made his way to Art, lifted his son to his feet, and pulled the duct tape from his mouth.

"Dad!" Art exclaimed. "The thieves . . . they were just . . ."

"They were just apprehended in the basement by a large number of police officers," his father said. Arthur Hamilton Sr. crouched down and started to tear the duct tape from Art's legs.

"But how?" Art asked.

Arthur Hamilton Sr. winked. "I got an alert from Soteria," he said. "Nicely done, by the way. The ammonia is what really caught my attention, particularly when the air filtration system couldn't seem to remove it. When I realized what was happening, I alerted security. They immediately covered all the exits—including the basement."

It worked! Art thought. Thank goodness for sweat.

But the ordeal wasn't over—not quite yet.

Art glanced around the room—he could see the director of the museum. He spotted the head of security. He saw several members of his father's staff, Catherine Dismuke, and the curator of the exhibit. Anyone who had anything to do with the exhibit was in the room—except for one particularly important person.

"Dad," Art said, "the people who did this are the same people who robbed the Gardner Museum."

To Art's surprise, his father did not laugh.

"That might be," his father replied, "but the men who were just arrested claim that they don't know who hired them. And unless you have more proof, there's not much we can do."

"The duct tape," Art replied. "That's the same way they tied up the guards at the Gardner Museum."

"Not enough," Art's father replied. "Everybody uses duct tape for everything. I'm sure these aren't the first criminals to use it."

Fair enough.

"They just tried to steal a Rembrandt, a Vermeer, a Degas, and a Manet—just like the Gardner theft," Art said.

Arthur Hamilton Sr. paused for a moment and then shook his head. "A coincidence," he replied.

"The Gardner Museum theft was almost exactly thirty years ago," Art noted.

This time his father paused a bit longer. The timing of the theft had clearly not occurred to him. "Strange," he finally said, "but it's not proof."

"There's one other thing," Art said.

Arthur Hamilton Sr. sighed. "Listen, you might be right," he said, "but I'm afraid that—"

"The yacht," Art interrupted.

"The yacht?" his father asked. "You mean the *Grognard*?"

"What is it with you and that boat?" Camille had been freed from the duct tape by her mother, and they had made their way over to join Art and his father.

"I didn't realize what the word *grognard* meant until Camille told me," Art said. "It's French—it means 'grumbler.'"

"What does that have to do with"—Camille waved her arms around—"all of this?"

Art smiled. "Grognard was also the nickname of a particular regiment of Napoleon's Imperial Guard."

Arthur Hamilton Sr.'s jaw dropped open. "It can't be!" he exclaimed.

"Yes," Art replied. "Is that enough proof?"

Arthur Hamilton Sr. did not respond. He turned to Camille and Mary Sullivan. He was clearly flustered. "My apologies," he said, "but I must . . . well . . . there's something that needs to be handled immediately."

And with that he sprinted across the room.

CHAPTER 57

6:51 p.m.

Saturday, April 23

National Portrait Gallery, Washington, DC

Mary Sullivan and Camille stared at Art.

"Okay," said Camille, "that was weird."

"Maybe a little more of an explanation for the rest of us?" Mary Sullivan asked.

Art nodded.

An explanation was probably in order—but where to start?

He turned to Camille. "Remember when I told you about the theft at the Isabella Stewart Gardner Museum?"

"They stole a half billion dollars' worth of art." Camille replied.

"I listened to a podcast about it," Mary Sullivan added. "It's hard to believe they stole all those paintings and got away with it."

"The thieves also took something else that night," Art said. "Something small that no one ever really talks about. They took a finial."

"A finial?" Camille asked. "What's a finial?"

"It's sort of a decoration that sits on top of a flagpole," Mary Sullivan replied. "Isn't that correct, Art?"

"That's right," Art said. "The thieves actually tried to take a flag that was hanging in the museum, but they couldn't get the flagpole off the wall. So they just took the finial on top of the flagpole instead. It was strange because no one could understand why they'd wanted the flag in the first place."

"I still don't get what that has to do with Napoleon . . . or *grognard*," Camille said, "or why your dad just ran off."

"The flag that the thieves tried to steal from the Gardner Museum," Art replied, "was a regimental flag from when Napoleon was emperor of France. Want to guess which regiment?"

"Are you kidding me?" Camille shouted. "It was the Grognard flag?"

Art nodded. "It was the Grognard flag," he said. "Mr. Hoggard's boat is named after the same regiment as the flag that the thieves tried to steal from the Gardner Museum. I don't think that is a coincidence."

It took a second for the news to sink in—and for the consequences to make themselves clear.

"Wait a second," Mary Sullivan said. "You think Mr. Hoggard had something to do with the Gardner Museum theft, don't you?"

A large smile appeared on Art's face.

"And the reason you figured that out was because I looked up the word *grognard*, right?" Camille asked. "I mean, I am the reason, right?"

Art tilted his head. "Ah . . . I suppose so," he replied.

"And so we wouldn't have come up here if I had not figured that out, right?" Camille said.

"Yep," Art replied.

"Cha-ching!" Camille pumped her fist. "Yes!" she exclaimed, and started dancing around the gallery.

Mary Sullivan looked at Art. "What's going on?" she asked. "And why is my daughter jumping around like a complete loon?"

Art laughed. "I told Camille about the reward for finding the paintings stolen from the Gardner Museum," Art replied. "Ten million dollars."

Mary Sullivan's eyes went wide. "Ten million dollars!" she exclaimed.

Art shrugged. "It won't be that easy. It could be years—lots of years—before the paintings are found, if they ever are. Most people think they were probably sold by the crooks who stole them. They could be anywhere on the planet. But at least it's a start."

Mary Sullivan smiled. "Then I suppose it wouldn't hurt to let her enjoy this for a bit."

CHAPTER 58

12:12 p.m.

Saturday, April 23

National Portrait Gallery, Washington, DC

It had been an exceedingly long night.

They sat in a conference room in the Lunder Conservation Center. Camille had her head down on the table. Her hair had finally burst free from its braid—it shot off in all directions across the table. Art felt as frazzled as Camille's hair looked.

They had completely missed the gala. They'd first had to get checked out by the medics to make sure they were okay—which they were. Then they had to sit through a series of interviews with the Metropolitan Police, the FBI, the Capitol Police, the Secret Service, and the head of security for the Smithsonian Institution. A representative from the Isabella Stewart Gardner Museum was already on his way to Washington, DC—they would meet with him tomorrow.

The FBI had apparently picked up Mr. Hoggard as he was heading toward the Wharf. He had already given instructions to his crew to set sail for international waters as soon as he arrived. The FBI was currently in the process of searching his yacht. Apparently Catherine Dismuke was completely legit—she'd had no idea that all of her work had been funneled by Mr. Hoggard to a set of art thieves on the side. The thieves, in turn, had no idea who had actually hired them. If Art and Camille had not managed to uncover the true meaning of *grognard,* then Mr. Hoggard would never have been caught.

Art yawned. It was now past midnight. His dad had said that they would be heading home soon—but that had been almost an hour ago.

"I wish my dad would hurry up," Art said.

Camille muttered something incoherent from beneath the mound of red hair piled on the opposite side of the table.

Art leaned back in his chair and closed his eyes. All of the paintings had been returned to the gallery, and the Millennium Exhibit would open as planned the following day. With all of the publicity from the night's events, the exhibit would probably draw even bigger crowds than anticipated. Word of the attempted theft had already hit all the major news outlets, and the connection to the Gardner Museum theft was being broadcast everywhere. Maybe there really was a chance of recovering some or all of the paintings that had been stolen thirty years ago.

Art allowed himself for the briefest of moments to consider what he would do if he and Camille actually did receive part of the reward from the Gardner Museum. It was fun to think about, but he suspected that he knew what his dad's response would be. Art might get to spend a little of it on something fun, but most of it would be saved for college or donated to some museum. He expected Mary Sullivan would feel the same way.

Art could feel himself starting to drift off to sleep. His eyelids had become heavy, and he found it difficult to keep his head upright. There was no sense in fighting the inevitable. He was just starting to put his head down on the table when there was a knock at the door.

The door creaked open, and Art's father stepped inside.

Maybe it was time to go home.

"There's one last person who wants to speak to you," his father said.

Art knew that what had happened at the museum was a really, really big deal—but he was also really, really tired.

"Can we do it tomorrow?" Art asked.

Arthur Hamilton Sr. shook his head. "I'm afraid not," he said. "But don't worry—this won't take long."

Art's father held the door open, and an older woman stepped into the room. She had white hair and wore a dark blue dress with a silver brooch. She carried a small purse that perfectly matched her dress.

Art immediately jumped up from his seat.

No way, he thought.

"Camille," Art said. "You need to wake up."

No response.

"Camille," Art repeated. "You really need to wake up."

"I just want to sleep," Camille muttered.

"You really, really need to wake up," Art repeated.

"Why do I need to wake up?" she muttered.

"Because I want to meet the young lady who saved the portrait of William Shakespeare," said Elizabeth II, the Queen of England, "and thank you on behalf of all of Great Britain."

Camille's head shot up from the table. Her eyes were wide, and her hair flew off in all directions.

"You have got to be kidding me," Camille said. She jumped up and tried to straighten her dress, which was now wrinkled beyond all belief.

"I'm not kidding," said the queen. "The whole world owes the two of you a great debt of gratitude."

Camille made her way from behind the table. A huge grin covered her face.

Art knew exactly what was coming.

Camille stood directly in front of the queen, bent slightly at the knees, and performed a perfect curtsy.

"Your Majesty," Camille said.

EPILOGUE

3:30 p.m.

Friday, June 19

Sullivan residence, Washington, DC

The final day of school.

Camille and Art made their way toward Camille's house for an afternoon of video games, television, and pizza. They were both looking forward to celebrating the last day of school, even though Art hated that the school year had come to an end. For the first time in his life, he had been surrounded on a daily basis by kids his own age, and he had loved it. Camille, however, had assured him that summer break was awesome — sleeping late, vacations, and no homework.

Art had completed his book report a week ago, and it had been reviewed and approved by both his father and Ms. Sullivan. Although there had been some adjustments to the punishments they had previously received, the book reports had still been required. Camille had, of course, protested the injustice of it all. However, after Mary Sullivan had shared with Camille how much had been charged on her credit card for them to use the scooter on that fateful day, Camille had quickly conceded the point. She had finished her book report the previous day, and it was currently under review. Art had little doubt that it would pass muster. Just reading a book that long was an accomplishment.

They made their way to Camille's house and dumped their backpacks by the door.

"We're home!" Camille yelled.

Mary Sullivan immediately appeared in the foyer. Her eyes were red—she appeared to have been crying.

"Mom!" Camille exclaimed. "What's wrong?"

Art didn't know what to say. He had never seen Ms. Sullivan like this. It was hard seeing someone so vulnerable. Art felt awkward and uncomfortable.

Mary Sullivan held a letter in her hand. "I received this letter this afternoon," she said. "I . . . almost threw it away."

"What is it?" Camille asked.

Mary Sullivan shook her head. "You just need to read it."

"Should I leave?" Art asked. He felt as if he was intruding into something that was intensely personal.

"No," Mary Sullivan replied. "Please stay."

Mary Sullivan handed the letter to her daughter.

Camille opened the letter and started reading. Art watched her face carefully, trying to draw any conclusions from her expressions. But Camille—whose facial expressions normally betrayed her every thought and emotion—remained remarkably stoic. She finished reading the letter, folded it neatly, and handed it back to her mother.

"The answer is yes," Camille said to her mother.

Her mother nodded and retreated from the room.

Camille turned to Art. A tear started running down her left cheek.

"That was a letter from my father."

"Your father?" Art exclaimed. "What does he want?"

Art knew Camille had never met her father.

Camille paused to compose herself. She took a deep breath and exhaled.

"He wants to meet me," she finally replied.

And with that, Camille broke down in tears. Art held his friend and hugged her as tightly as he could.

AUTHOR'S NOTE

The theft of thirteen works of art from the Isabella Stewart Gardner Museum on March 18, 1990, really happened —and in pretty much the way described in the prologue to this book. The thieves really did dress as police officers. They really did spend eighty-one minutes in the museum. And they really did steal the finial that sat on top of the flagpole.

The works stolen were the following:

Chinese gu (twelfth century BCE)

Christ in the Storm on the Sea of Galilee by Rembrandt van Rijn (1633)

A Lady and Gentleman in Black by Rembrandt van Rijn (1633)

Portrait of the Artist as a Young Man by Rembrandt van Rijn (c. 1633)

Landscape with an Obelisk by Govaert Flinck (1638)

The Concert by Johannes Vermeer (1663–1666)

Leaving the Paddock by Edgar Degas (nineteenth century)

Eagle finial by Antoine-Denis Chaudet (1813–1814)

Procession on a Road near Florence by Edgar Degas (1857–1860)

Chez Tortoni by Édouard Manet (c. 1875)

Study for the Programme 1 by Edgar Degas (1884)

Study for the Programme 2 by Edgar Degas (1884)

Three Mounted Jockeys by Edgar Degas (c. 1885–1888)

These works of art have not been seen since. No one has ever been arrested. No suspects have ever been formally identified. And a ten-million-dollar reward really does exist.

Of course, there have been lots of rumors and speculation over the course of the past thirty years. There is a brilliant podcast from WBUR public radio called *Last Seen* about what happened, the rumors surrounding the theft, and the long list of possible suspects. But I'll spoil the ending of the podcast for you—we still don't know where the paintings are or who stole them.

There may be a tendency and a temptation—as time passes—to mythicize what occurred at the Gardner Museum. Perhaps there will be a box-office film one day, the thieves turned into lovable rogues who pulled off the impossible heist. But I invite the reader to visit Boston and take a visit to the Isabella Stewart Gardner Museum. I invite you to go see the empty frames hanging on the walls. It is not a myth. It is very real. The world has been deprived of works of art by some of the greatest painters that history has bestowed upon us.

But hope remains.

Perhaps one day someone will stumble upon something somewhere that leads to a real clue as to where these priceless works of art may be.

Best wishes, and good luck.

Deron R. Hicks

Warm Springs, Georgia

UNLOCK THE SECRETS OF THE
LOST ART MYSTERIES

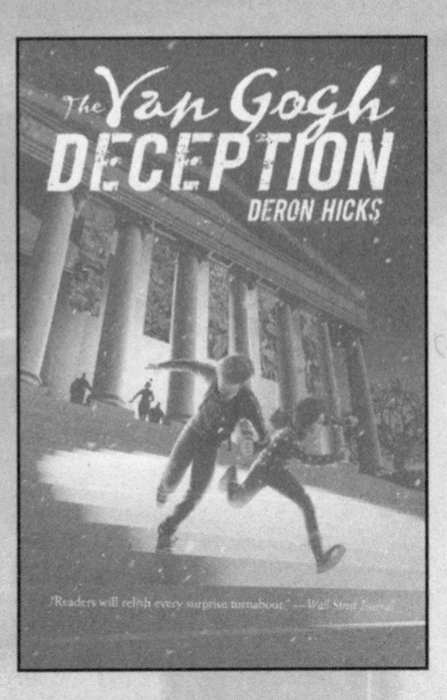